The Devil
of
Dragon House

The Devil
of
Dragon House

Janis Susan May

A Judy Sullivan Book
Walker and Company
New York

To
Angelica
Justin and Benjamin
Judith and Paul Bryan
Maile and Travis
Tancy
and all the other little and once little ones
who have so enriched my life, this book is lovingly
dedicated.

First published in the United States of America in 1985 by the Walker Publishing Company, Inc.

Published simultaneously in Canada by John Wiley & Sons Canada, Limited, Rexdale, Ontario.

Library of Congress Cataloging in Publication Data

May, Janis Susan, 1946–
    The devil of Dragon House.

    "A Judy Sullivan book."
    1. Title.
PS3563.A9418D4 1985   813'.54   85-652
ISBN 0-8027-0843-9
Printed in the United States of America

10 9 8 7 6 5 4 3 2

Chapter One

MY FATHER DIED some weeks before my birth while trying to take a ridiculously high fence. My mother lingered after him only long enough to insure my entry into the world. Father left me an excellent name and little else, and so it was my lot to be passed from one portion of his large and illustrious southern family to another, never remaining with any of them long enough for the most unladylike strength of mind and self-determination developed in this process to become apparent. Like the wild creatures I loved, I learned to create a good camouflage and passed into young adulthood in the disguise of a quiet and somewhat bookish female who was quite content to sit in the background while my livelier cousins flirted and laughed with the sons of the local gentry. I can imagine the haughty Farradays thought it was because I knew my place as a poor relation. I am sure they would have been quite shocked to find that my reticence came not from propriety but from boredom.

In my years of wandering from relation to relation, I had learned the necessity of adapting—as much as my pride and temper would allow—to their differing ways and notions. Uncle Henry and Aunt Ida had been strong Temperance workers and had seen to it that I signed the Pledge as soon as I was able to write; but when Aunt Ida had become ill with the dropsy, I had been sent to Uncle Miller and Aunt Belle where it was the custom for even the smallest children to take well-watered wine at dinner. Uncle Miller said good palates were begun young: to refuse was to be mercilessly teased and berated, so I drank.

It was like that my whole life. Great-aunt Pearl was a rabid horsewoman, so I was expected to learn how to ride—which I did and liked—and Great-aunt Lorena was a blue-stocking who valued learning above anything. I think I liked living with her best; had she lived I probably would have stayed with her in that tiny house in Savannah, reading aloud to her as her eyes failed, until I became the spinster Miss Farraday of Azalea Street. If that had happened, however, I should have no tale to tell and would have never experienced the odd blend of terror and delight that has been my lot.

Yet Great-aunt Lorena did die, and I was sent to the last and perhaps the wealthiest of the Farradays, my father's older brother Richard and his wife Evelyn. They lived at the family plantation, Moonhaven, and had two daughters approximately my age. It would have seemed that they should have been the natural ones to take me in the first place, for in a household with a small army of slaves the addition of one newborn infant to the nursery could make scant difference, but Aunt Evelyn refused to countenance my presence until every other alternative had been exhausted and I was of an age to be useful to her and her girls.

For years I had agonized over her coolness, trying to find its origin in something I had done unwittingly, until quite by accident I happened to learn that Aunt Evelyn had been the belle of the county and had loved my father to distraction. He had surprised her by returning from a business trip to New York with a bride. It was more than Aunt Evelyn could bear. To lose a beau was bad enough, but to lose him to a Yankee and then be expected to bring up the child of that union . . . I could almost hear her complaining to Uncle Richard, who always listened patiently and agreed to her every comment.

Poor Aunt Evelyn! Stuck with me at last, at a time by which I had perfected my disguise, she was unable to find fault except in one regard—one that I was unable to hide or change—my hair. It is, I'm told, my mother's hair—thick, wavy, and the color of fresh-shined copper. Thus Aunt Evelyn's dissatisfaction with the larger situation came to rest upon my head.

Only one other feature of my life at that time is worth mentioning, for in retrospect it is the most important. So far I have only mentioned my father's family, for it was they who raised me, but my mother was not without kin; she had a sister and a niece almost my age. Even if my Farraday relatives had considered the possibility of sending me to my mother's people in the cold and alien North, my cousin Dorothea was no better off than I. Orphaned before the age of six by a carriage accident, she had been consigned to the care of her father's sister.

I forget just how my existence came to her notice; my first inkling that I had any relations beyond the numerous Farradays was when Dorothea's letter came. At the time, I was living with Uncle Miller and Aunt Belle and was desperately unhappy; the letter from my unknown cousin seemed a heaven-sent omen that there was a life beyond the close confines of Farraday blood.

We corresponded passionately. I told Dorothea of the humdrum line of my life, which she charmingly thought interesting, and she told me of her exciting life in the Connecticut village of Port Harmon. Her letters seemed like novels, full of winter skating parties, of the romance of the sailing ships coming in, laden with trade goods from China and the mysterious East, or of the more prosaic whalers with their casks of oil. Once she wrote of a trip to New York for shopping; her aunt even allowed her to attend a performance of Shakespeare at one of the theatres. Dorothea lamented that her aunt would not permit her to see anything more exciting. I thought it wonderful; my experiences with the theatre had been the traveling showboat which gave the same tired old melodramas continually and Aunt Belle's Poetry Society readings every other Thursday evening.

All in all, my cousin Dorothea seemed to be a privileged creature from another world; even her name was exotic when compared to my own dull Drusilla. I hated my own name so much that finally, in the way of young girls, we coined private nicknames; she became Doro—she said in Italian that meant "of gold"—and by some strange metamorphosis I became Dilly. Of course my letters were routinely read by Aunt Belle and then by Great-aunt Pearl as was the custom, but no one else ever picked up the habit of calling me anything but Drusilla, usually followed by "you ungrateful girl." Great-aunt Lorena thought it an unwarranted invasion of privacy to read another's letters and Aunt Evelyn didn't seem to care what I did, as long as it didn't interfere with the pleasure or advancement of her girls, so for some time my correspondence had been my own.

It was a good thing, for in the last months of my stay at Moonhaven, Doro fell in love. Apparently I was her only confidante, for her letters detailed every word of their conversations, every moment they spent together. With some alarm, I read of how her beloved Mr. Berkley courted her with a singlemindedness that was almost overwhelming, vowing her to speak of him to no one as there were hideous unnamed forces dedicated to keeping them apart. It was as fantastic as any novel, and dear Doro believed every word. I, of course, wrote advising caution, but her next letter was written earlier and must have crossed mine in the mail. There were to be no others.

Even in 1858 there was much concern about northern encroachment against our southern way of life, and, on occasion, the topic of war would creep into conversations. My cousins Flora and Eula would squeal with terror and vow to the heavens that they would not know what to do if such a calamity should occur, thus giving the gentlemen opportunity to reassure them in the best masculine form, namely, hand-holding, looking deeply into their eyes, and—if they were very sure that Aunt Evelyn was not about—a sweetly stolen kiss.

One particular afternoon I had joined the party, having been turned out of my usual refuge in the library and told by a beaming Aunt Evelyn to go and be sociable with the young people, most especially with an extremely boring young preacher who was her distant kin on her father's side. Dutifully I tried to engage the Reverend Mr. Entwhistle in conversation, but, aside from quoting enormous chunks of scripture verbatim, he seemed incapable of communication and finally drifted away to join a group of other social misfits in a desultory game of horseshoes.

I have often wondered that if I had known then what was to come from the Reverend Mr. Entwhistle's departure, would I have let him go so easily? Perhaps it is a blessing that the knowledge of the future is denied us, for we are weak and pliable creatures.

Following my long tradition of quiet disassociation, I walked a little way from the crowd and sat down on the old porch swing. My billowing summer muslin skirts covered nearly the entire seat, and I had to bunch them up most uncomfortably when Jack Howard asked if he might join me.

Jack was the son of a planter and quite the catch of the county. I had never thought of him in a romantic light, having been told time and time again that he was earmarked for Flora, but he was intelligent, and we had quite serious conversations on occasion. He treated me as his intellectual equal, and I spared him the vaporish nattering expected from a female, an arrangement guaranteed to preclude any romantic attachment according to Aunt Evelyn.

When he sat down beside me that sunny September afternoon and asked me if I thought there would indeed be a war, I had no idea of his intentions. When I answered yes, that unless policies changed soon there would undoubtedly be some sort of martial conflict, no one could have been more surprised than I when he flung himself to his knees and begged for my hand in marriage before he should have to heed the call to arms. Had it been in a more private place I might have been able to dissuade him and keep the whole affair quiet, but his choice of the porch at Moonhaven during a sociable afternoon made it a public occasion.

My memory of the next few hours is hazy. I do remember Aunt Evelyn shouting at me that I was an ungrateful girl to take their bread and shelter while trying to steal my cousin's beau. Flora was whimpering, calling me a silent snake-in-the-grass, and Eula, who had lost nothing, howled just to keep up the chorus. Uncle Richard took refuge in the billiard room with his brandy decanter as was his habit at the first sign of something unpleasant. Jack was dismissed with a highly colored view of my actions, all designed to make me look bad and Flora good. Though to his credit, I'll always think that he didn't believe a word of it, even when Aunt Evelyn told him that I was all but engaged to the Reverend Mr. Entwhistle.

When I hotly denied my engagement, not from any affection for Jack Howard but from a wish to vindicate my taste, Aunt Evelyn told me that she had been considering my future and had decided that marriage with the Oregon-bound preacher was the best thing for me. That had been the purpose behind his visit. In her generosity, Aunt Evelyn was even going to give me a wedding at Moonhaven and a small dowry in addition to the inheritance Great-aunt Lorena had left me. I left the room in a towering rage, my oft-suppressed temper blowing free at last.

It was only later, after a tearful session in my room, that I began to think seriously about my future. Aunt Evelyn was serious; she had every intention of seeing me married to the Entwhistle man and docilely disappearing into Oregon. After the episode of Jack Howard, she would be doubly determined.

With trembling hands, I lit a candle and re-read Doro's last letter. Her romantic tête-à-têtes with her beloved Mr. Berkley now sounded both secure and enviable; at least she had one person who loved her. With the exception of Great-aunt Lorena, I had never felt loved in my life, except for Doro, of course, and she was so far away.

> *. . . oh, dearest Dilly, I cannot tell you how happy I am! My dear Mr. Berkley and I met this afternoon at the lending library and had almost an hour together! He kissed my hand, saying that he looked forward to the time he had the right to kiss my lips. . . .*

It sounded heavenly to feel so happy about someone, though I could imagine no such rapture at being kissed by Jack or the reverend. Perhaps I was incapable of feeling the passions of the world? It was a depressing thought on a depressing evening.

> *. . . Mr. Berkley asked me again if I had mentioned meeting him to anyone and I of course said I had not (I saw no reason to mention my correspondence with you, dearest Dilly, for surely to write is not the same thing as to speak and in any event you are too far away to provide him with any worry). . . . Oh,*

how I look forward to being able to invite you to stay at my own home, Devon House. I have not yet seen it, but he says it is unbelievably beautiful and I shall be there before long. Apparently he is about to conquer the evil forces which conspire against him and will soon be able to acknowledge our love in the light; it will be wonderful to be his fiancée openly, but I own I shall miss the excitement of our stolen moments, for nothing could be sweeter. I wish you could be as happy as I, dear Dilly, my own beloved cousin. . . .

There was more, but I had read enough to give me my escape. I would run to Doro! She would give me shelter until I was able to set myself up in some sort of gainful employment. I dare not stay at Moonhaven, for even if the Reverend Mr. Entwhistle were banished, someone else equally odious would surely take his place. Even to go down to the family's reproachful faces tomorrow would be painful.

Then it must be tonight!

I planned to travel light, taking the only two pitiful pieces of jewelry Mother left me, my father's watch, and his miniature in a locket. For clothing, I took the minimum of unmentionables, a nightgown, two of my sturdiest winter dresses, and an extra pair of shoes. I tied these and my toilet articles together in my winter cloak and shawl. It made an unwieldy bundle, but I dared not risk a trip to the attic for my battered basket trunk. I had but one dark bonnet; thank heavens it was inconspicuous and drab.

Money was my second consideration. I had never held more than a dollar in my hands at any given time in my life. Which is not to say that I didn't know the value of money; Great-aunt Lorena had seen that I knew the basics of economics, from national down to household, and I knew I could not get to Connecticut without a fair sum. My next actions were not ones I remember with pride, but I say to this day it was not stealing. Indeed I did break into Aunt Evelyn's desk and take five hundred dollars, and although there are some who would regard this as theft, I was really only reclaiming that which was mine. Great-aunt Lorena had left me her entire estate—much to the pique of Aunt Evelyn—and Uncle Richard had taken charge of it, keeping it in trust for me. I was never quite sure of its amount, but I'm positive it was more than five hundred dollars. In any event, my conscience was quite clear, almost as clear as that dazzling moonlit night in my seventeenth year when I crept away from Moonhaven, from the Farradays, from all that I had ever known to seek a better life for myself.

What I found . . . ah, but I jump ahead of my narrative.

Chapter Two

I DID MAKE it to Connecticut safely, though not without a share of adventures and indignities; suffice it to say that it is a shame in this modern era that a woman is unable to travel alone without being submitted to stares and impertinences which would not be considered if she were with a companion. Apparently, that Stanton woman's female rights convention ten years before had hindered attitudes between the sexes here in the North instead of helped them.

It was just past sunset when the tiny train finally puffed into the little Port Harmon station some six hours late, due to a tree most inconsiderately falling across the rails and other assorted disasters of a minor nature. I had not really objected to the delays, for they gave me an opportunity to study more closely this unyielding land of forest and stone, until our late arrival brought my predicament sharply home. Here I was in the same town at last with Doro, but I had to find her or I had no place to stay that night. Besides that, it was only September but it was cold. For the past two days of travel, I had huddled in my heaviest winter dress and cloak, unable to warm my sun-starved blood; if it were this cold in early autumn, what must the winters be like?

Keeping my veil lowered to discourage the stares of the curious—I had purchased it early in the journey for just that purpose—I approached the only thing appearing to be public transportation, namely a strange combination of buggy and spring-wagon presided over by an even stranger man.

"Are you for hire?"

He nodded, a queer jerking motion as if he were manipulated by strings. "Happen I am. Luggage?"

I handed him my small bundle, now protected only by my shawl, and waited for him to assist me into his curious vehicle; I waited in vain, for he merely tossed my things in the back and climbed into the driver's seat, leaving me to scramble up the best I could. The New England countryside might be beautiful, but the manners of its inhabitants left much to be desired.

"Where to?"

"The home of Miss Conroe, on Millington Street. I believe it is number thirty-six."

The driver nodded and clicked to his horse; I breathed a tired sigh, thinking my long journey almost over, picturing my joyous meeting with Doro at last and, although it shows the basic selfishness of my nature, a most appealing cup of tea. The chill had intensified and despite myself I shivered. I could see little of the town in the scant light, except that it appeared mean and drab. Such an impression was depressing and I resolved to forget it.

My spirits received another blow when we at last arrived at 36 Millington Street. Doro had described the house to me, a two-storied clapboard with white paint and green shingles and a stained-glass fanlight over the front door. This was the house, though it was smaller than I had pictured it, but the shutters were locked and the entire place dark. In the feeble light of the driver's lantern, an air of desolation hung over the house like a cloud.

"It's empty!" I wailed and to my irritation I sounded both lost and desperate. "No one's there." For a sinking moment, I almost wished myself back at Moonhaven. The acerbic voice of the driver transformed my self-pity to anger.

"Of course it is; happen old Miss Conroe's been gone this last month or more. Gone to Boston, they say."

"Gone? There's no one here at all?"

"Nay, nary a soul. House be shuttered for the winter."

"You knew this? You brought me all the way out here and didn't tell me?" My voice had reached a most unlady-like volume, but by then I was not feeling very much like a lady.

"Happen you didn't ask me."

I am proud of my reaction, for neither did I strike him nor regale him with a string of epithets I had no business knowing. Instead of indulging in such worthless and selfish excesses, I forced myself to breathe deeply and think. My situation was not enviable and my choices were limited.

"It were because of that niece of hers," the man offered and noisily deposited a large lump of spittle on the street below.

"Doro? Miss Dorothea, I mean? What happened?"

Apparently he liked to gossip, for he settled back and prepared to enjoy his story. "Conroe's always been a respected family name in these parts; old Miss Conroe's father was one of the town's leading citizens and Miss Conroe herself did more than her share of good works."

He was enjoying this! I bit my lips.

"No, never thought the young miss would turn out like that, for all her pert ways. Running off in the middle of the night, just like she were some dockside trollop. Proves she were no better than she had ought to be."

"She ran off?"

"Ran off. Left her aunt a note she was going to be married and she'd be back in a few days but she never showed up, as if anyone expected her to. Miss Conroe swore up and down her niece had been kidnapped, said the girl didn't even have a beau, started a whole hue and cry, but of course nothing came of it. Them quiet ones are the ones you have to watch." He chuckled reminiscently and made soft sucking sounds against his few remaining teeth.

My dark horizon began to lighten. I knew what had happened; Doro and her beloved Mr. Berkley had eloped and by the time it was safe—from whatever danger he feared—Doro's aunt had already left for Boston. Doubtlessly Doro had already made her peace with her aunt, but the old lady had decided for her own reasons not to return and enlighten the town of Port Harmon just yet. Well, that was their duty and not mine. I would keep silent and let them tell the story in their own good time. I knew where Doro was.

The little man was regarding me appraisingly; he had told the story and now probably expected some information in return. I suppose I presented somewhat of a figure of mystery, arriving late at night, swathed in veils and asking to be taken to an empty house.

"Be you a relative?"

"In a way," I murmured.

"Surprised you didn't know any of this. You're not from these parts."

"No."

"Brave or foolish, that's what you are, traveling by yourself during these times."

"My trip was not difficult."

"I didn't mean your trip, young lady. You do be a young one, don't ye? Can't fool me when it comes to voices. A young woman's voice is like no other." He laughed, displaying a stubbled set of gums. "It's a brave young woman who travels alone along the Shauquatuck coast these days."

"Brave? Why? Are you trying to tell me something?"

He laughed again, but this time it was sinister. "Am I trying to tell you something, young woman? Just what every Christian in this part of the country knows. The Devil is walking abroad these nights and no young woman would be alone for anything in the world."

I could not help a small giggle. Aunt Evelyn had often spoken disparagingly about the Yankees' over-righteous Calvinist attitudes towards religion, but I had dismissed it as a prejudice against my mother's people.

"The Devil? In Connecticut?"

"Aye! You laugh, but ten young ladies who have disappeared in the last four months aren't laughing. Not one of them left any note, neither. One minute they're there and the next they're not. They're gone where no one can find or help them."

"Ten young women are missing? Has nothing been done to locate them?"

"Aye, they searched—beat every bush in the woods, they did, every time one of them went, but it did no good. Old Dan Scratch intends to keep what he takes. Well, young woman, are we going to sit here all night and wait for him to come and get you, or shall I take you back to town? Old Mother Harrington runs a respectable boarding house."

He was trying to be kind. Although I dismissed his tale of the Devil ambling through the countryside picking up unsuspecting young maidens, it did provoke a certain shudder, as it was a story best told and laughed at while surrounded by family and friends. A dark, chilly night with only a cackling gnome for company was no time for ghost stories!

"Do you know," I asked slowly, wondering how best to serve myself and protect Doro's secret, "a residence called Devon House?"

The driver started so suddenly that the horse, aware of his master's shaking hands on the rein, stamped his hooves and shook his head. In the still darkness, broken only by the feeble glow of the wagon's lantern, the jingle of the harness sounded incongruously gay.

"Devon House?" he repeated and made a curious sign with his left hand. "The only place called Devon House in this area be that built by the accursed Captain Berkley down the coast a way, near Jefferson."

Berkley. The name of Doro's beloved confirmed my theory, but the driver's reaction was far from reassuring. "That," I said with more resolution than I felt, "is where I wish to go."

"Not in my wagon, you don't; I'd not go anywhere near that place after dark for all the tea in China!"

I took a deep breath; this evening was not turning out at all the way I had planned. "I'll double your usual fee," I said recklessly.

Fear and greed wrestled in his eyes. Aunt Evelyn had often spoken disparagingly of the Yankees' love of gold; I do not know if it is a regional trait or not, but it certainly worked with the little man, for he spoke at last, rushing the words together as if to get them out before he changed his mind.

"Very well, I'll take you there, but only to the gate; I'll go no nearer that heathen house." Then he named a sum which I privately thought closer to four or five times his normal fee, but which I agreed to pay when I was safely deposited at Devon House. Then I had every intention of shaming him into taking me to the door.

13

Such tactics didn't work, as I found out, for after what seemed to be hours and hours of riding, he stopped before an enormous stone gate and refused to go one step further. Even the threat of no pay at all left him unmoved, and he touchingly offered to take me back to town for free if only I would not enter that house. I almost weakened, for no building at all could be seen from the gate, but the thought of a happy and welcoming Doro just a short way away firmed my resolution and increased my pique with this stubborn man. Eventually I paid him the price upon which we had agreed, took my bundle, and forged down that shadowy lane, barely illuminated by the thin moon and nearly covered over with trees. The sound of the sea, never distant, dogged my steps with its monotonous rhythm.

I tried to tell myself that it was only the dark, the driver's scary tales, and the road's disrepair that made my path seem so sinister. I picked myself up from yet another stumble. At last I did reach the house—for endless, dark walks exist only in nightmares—but the prospect was unappealing. It was a big place, but somehow forbidding and closed-in. There were a minimum of tiny windows and no outside decorations, save the ever-present utilitarian shutters; the grounds were wild, with only the barest hint of a lawn and almost no shrubbery, giving the house a naked, alien look.

Had things been more normal, I surely would have given some thought to my appearance. It was not my habit to appear unannounced with bonnet awry, dress muddied, and hair every which-a-way, but by now all I wanted was to see Doro, give her husband a few stern words on the condition of his drive, and then fall asleep for a great number of hours. No part of my lengthy journey from Georgia had been more taxing than this last few hours.

At least some of the windows were still lighted. I grabbed at a queerly carved handle—its true shape undistinguishable in the darkness—and pulled. Somewhere deep in the house a bell tolled.

I think had the door not been answered I would have given up, curling into a ball on the doorstep and sleeping there until dawn came with renewing warmth and light, but such drastic measures were not necessary. The narrow window beside the door showed the glow of an approaching light and in a moment the portal opened.

The light from the lamp was dazzling after the dark outside, but I could see well enough to know that the face staring into mine was yellow and masklike, wearing an inscrutable expression that gave way to one of horror before the odd creature turned and hurriedly scuttled away.

Chapter Three

SOMEWHAT BEMUSED, I stepped inside the hall and closed the door behind me. The lamp the poor creature had left still burned on a nearby table, but it hardly illuminated the gloom, and the interior of the house was almost as chill as the outside.

My actions may sound heroic and brave, but I assure you they were neither; I was merely too tired to await the amenities. Had I never seen a Chinaman before I can only suppose that my reaction would have been different, but years ago one of Great-aunt Lorena's friends had had a Chinese serving-woman who proved to be both gentle and kind to a lonely little girl. I never knew quite how she came to be living in Savannah, for whenever the subject of her past came up between the elderly ladies I was ordered from the room.

That did not, however, explain why the servant was so afraid of me; had I been thinking clearly it would surely have seemed odd that a servant in an American household should be so alarmed at another American—however disheveled and unkempt I might be— but at the moment I was merely glad to have reached my destination at last.

How little I knew.

"Chang? Was that the front door? Who'd come calling at this time of night? Chang! Where are you, you damned nuisance?"

To describe the words as a bellow would be to do them a disservice; they seemed to be like a thunderclap or rockfall, something as powerful as the earth's elements themselves. He strode into the hallway, and for one wild moment I almost believed the old driver's tales of the Devil walking in Connecticut; this man could have been the Prince of Darkness.

The first impression was of darkness; in the shadowy hallway his hair appeared sooty, his black suit fading to nothingness. His brows were straight dark slashes in a hawkish face, that might have been hewn from a strong marble, only slightly less pallid than the snowy collar which encircled his neck. Eyes that were nothing but gleaming pools of darkness under the shadowing brows swept me with a gaze that felt like ice water. The only color was a half-healed scar on his cheek; its vibrant purplish red seemed to have drawn all life and vitality from his being.

Try as I would, I could not picture my cousin Doro writing with such passion about this harsh-featured man. Proximity to such intensity was uncomfortable, and I found myself shifting from foot to foot like some half-witted house girl under the force of his gaze.

"If Chang is the man-servant who answered the door, he ran that way."

"Lazy devil never was worth anything, but it's hard to picture him running away. You do look bad enough to scare anyone, though."

"That, sir," I replied testily, "can hardly be considered my fault. Between the refusal of my driver to bring me any further than your gates and the condition of your road, it is a miracle I am still in one piece!" All I had heard about the Yankees' lack of gallantry was obviously true.

"No one comes near this place after dark," he said, moving more into the light. It was a distinct shock to see that he limped and used a cane; such intensity marred by infirmity was startling.

"I am Miss Farraday," I answered his unspoken question. "I should like to see Mrs. Berkley."

His graven countenance did not alter. "It is an unusual time of night to be making a social call, Miss Farraday."

How rude the creature was to chatter on and leave me in ignorance of his identity. Did Yankees have no manners at all?

"I know that and I apologize, but the choice of time was not my own. First the train was delayed, and then there was a discussion with the driver."

He was nodding. "Yes, the rail service seems to get worse every day. That's as may be, however; still, it is late and my mother has already retired for the evening. She enjoys poor health. Might I help you instead?"

So he was a Berkley: it was not inconceivable. He certainly acted like the lord of the manor.

"You misunderstand me. I am looking for my cousin who used to be Miss Dorothea Conroe."

Somethng flickered in the pools of his eyes. "Won't you come into the library, Miss Farrington, was it?"

"Farraday," I corrected, but he was already limping down the dark hallway, taking my obedience for granted. Irritating as such high-handed measures were, it seemed I would have to follow him if only to inform him of just what I thought about his manners.

Fortunately for him, the sight of the library drove all such thoughts from my mind. The lighting was quite bright in this large chamber, so much so that the strangely carved furniture seemed to leap out. Scaly creatures writhed on chair arms and chest fronts, their eyes bulging and, in some cases, most realistically painted. Impressions hit me in waves. The room was lined with books, but they were covered with dust. The entire room, in fact, was layered with accumulated dirt and looked as if it had been sealed for a generation and only just now reopened. However, the desk, fantastically carved from some exotic reddish wood, was scrupulously clean and piled with neat stacks of papers and ledgers. The surprisingly utilitarian inkstand was open; apparently I had interrupted a bookkeeping session.

"Please sit down, Miss Farraday," he said, stationing himself behind the big desk and indicating a nearby chair.

It was dusty, but my clothing's condition was worse, and frankly I was so tired that in a moment or two I should have sat on the floor. In the brilliant light of the library, I started to get an idea of exactly how disheveled I did look; great splashes of mud adorned my skirts and my hands were filthy. I removed the dangling bonnet and began to attempt a straightening of the rats' nest my hair had become.

"You will forgive me if I seem a bit overwhelmed, Miss Farraday, and I hope you will forgive my bad manners as well. I am Nicholas Berkley. You said something about your cousin." He spoke tensely, moving his jaw as little as possible, probably to ease the half-healed wound on his cheek. Try as I might, I could not help staring at it.

"The former Miss Dorothea Conroe. I believe she is now mistress of this house."

Mr. Berkley's laugh was harsh. "There is no mistress of Devon House, Miss Farraday. Surely you can see that by the squalor that surrounds you?"

It seemed that all my years of practice at holding my tongue were for naught, for I blurted "You said your mother—"

"My mother is an invalid." A darkling look passed over his features, and the words came out as mere slivers. He shook his head slightly before turning back to me with a benign look, if one can call such villainous features benign. "This young lady you mentioned . . ."

"Miss Dorothea Conroe."

"I can assure you that no young lady, married or otherwise, resides at Devon House." His voice took on a musing tone. "Dorothea Conroe—that name sounds familiar."

How embarrassing it was to have to discuss my cousin's private affairs with this man and yet, I never had a thought about not telling him. Despite his piratical appearance, Mr. Nicholas Berkley had the gift of inspiring confidence. Or perhaps I was so weary and disappointed, it was easier to believe his protestations of innocence than not.

"She eloped from her home in Port Harmon some weeks ago. I believe her aunt disbelieved her story and raised a hue and cry."

He nodded. "I remember now. The constable called here to ask if we knew anything about it; said he was making a canvas of every house in the area. She was never found, was she? Well, Miss Farraday, what made you think you'd find your cousin here?"

"She wrote me," I said simply. "Doro said she was in love with a Mr. Berkley of Devon House. When I found out that she had eloped, I naturally assumed . . ."

The door burst inward without ceremony, banging sharply against the long table and setting a figurine to dancing dangerously.

"Nicholas! Chang has just told me the most fantastic story. . . ."

Obviously the newcomer was quite closely related to Mr. Berkley, for at first glance they appeared to have come from the same mold; at least, they would have, had Nicholas Berkley been in the same bloom of health as this gentleman. Similar in height, he was more muscular than my host, but the dark hair and eyes were identical except the newcomer bore no scar and his skin was ruddy with good health. And yet, there was a difference: where Nicholas Berkley was all fine-hewn angles and edges, this gentlemen seemed to be softer, less harsh, as if a slightly blurred version of Mr. Berkley.

He stopped in mid-step and stared, his complexion rapidly changing color. "I say! Chang told me that a red-haired devil had come to the house. I thought he had just been nipping at brandy again."

"I am already aware that my appearance is enough to scare little children, but such circumstances are beyond my control, and I think it very rude of you to make such sport of my condition!"

The unfortunate gentleman, perhaps unused to being so scourged by a female, took a step backward and almost onto the wide-eyed Chang, who had been dogging his footsteps. Then, surprisingly, Nicholas Berkley filled the room with a loud and rusty laugh.

"Bravo, Miss Farraday. I keep telling my brother his manners are totally beyond recall; perhaps he only needed a stronger medicine. May I present my younger brother, Simon Berkley. Simon, this is Miss Farraday—have you a Christian name, Miss Farraday?" His eyes were alight with unholy amusement, giving his face a surprising animation.

"Drusilla."

Simon Berkley bowed over my hand with as much grace as any of our southern beaux. "I do beg your pardon, Miss Drusilla Farraday. Please believe me I meant no harm nor insult. It is just that certain sects among the Chinese believe that demons have red hair, and they use that description to cover almost any unusual occurrence. To actually find . . ." He shrugged elegantly. "We are not used to such pleasant surprises at Devon House. Please forgive my gaucherie."

I am only flesh and blood and such a pretty apology, supported by such dark eyes, could not be refused.

"And I must ask you to overlook my quick temper, sir. It has been a difficult day."

"Indeed it has for all of us, Miss Farraday," Nicholas said, and I sensed layers of meaning in his innocuous comment. "Simon, Miss Farraday comes to us with a most wondrous tale. But first . . ." Here he turned to the servant Chang and spoke rapidly with a series of sounds that seemed closer to bird calls than human language.

Then a queer thing happened, so quickly I was not sure of having seen it myself. Nicholas Berkley had given his attention back to me, but Chang had turned to Simon Berkley in a questioning manner, and Simon had given a barely perceptible nod before the soft-footed servant finally turned to go. Perhaps it meant nothing, perhaps it had not even happened. Heaven knows I was far from being alert at the moment. In fact, in my weariness and confusion, it almost seemed that the carved dragons on the tall chest were beginning to move.

"They are excellent examples of wood-carving, aren't they?" Simon had followed my gaze. His pride was obvious. "Beautiful! They almost look alive."

"A little too much so for my taste. I think them hideous." My accursed tongue again! "The craftsmanship is obviously superior, though."

Nicholas Berkley was smiling—a painful, lopsided exercise—at my obvious discomfort. "Don't be embarrassed, Miss Farraday. Chinese art is an acquired taste."

His brother's face was expressionless. "Have you never seen Chinese art before, then?"

"No—it's—" I looked around the room and searched for an appropriate word. "It's a little overwhelming."

"I suppose so," Simon replied easily and then broke out with a sunny smile of singular beauty. "We've lived with this most of our lives. It must be rather startling if you aren't prepared for it.

Nicholas, what were you talking about earlier, about the lovely Miss Farraday bringing us a wondrous tale?"

Nicholas looked up at his brother, now perched gracefully on the edge of the desk, and once again I felt currents I could not fathom. "She is under the impression that her cousin Dorothea Conroe is the chatelaine of Devon House, having married a Mr. Berkley."

Simon's astonishment was almost comical. "The Devil! I say, Nicholas, you haven't a pretty young bride stashed away, have you? Dorothea Conroe . . ."

"The young lady who disappeared some weeks ago. Constable Bulwer called by not long after—after I was brought home." His voice hesitated just the slightest bit; were his infirmities then of a recent origin?

"I remember. What makes you think your—cousin, was it?— might be here?"

"She wrote me all about her courtship," I replied slowly. Weariness was sinking in on me like a wave, pulling me under into restful blackness. "Please tell me if Doro is here or not."

"Miss Farraday, I can give you my word that Miss Dorothea Conroe is not in this house and, to my knowledge, never has been." Somehow Nicholas had gotten across the room and the dragons were gone, replaced by a row of glinting bottles. "Simon, would you go up and see how Chang is doing? Here, Miss Farraday, drink this. You look absolutely white."

Apparently glad of his chance, Simon left the room. I took the glass Nicholas pressed into my chilled fingers and drained it without question, only to exclaim "Napoleon brandy!" as the fiery liquid literally brought me back to consciousness with a jolt.

"You know about spirits?" He sounded startled.

"An uncle of mine was something of a connoisseur," I murmured. The brandy had indeed brought about a resurgence of rational thought and—it is with some shame that I confess—my first thoughts were of my own immediate future rather than the mystery of my missing cousin Doro. "Mr. Berkley . . ."

Nicholas waved a languid hand; it was thin and white, but even in its emaciated state it spoke of strength. "Please, Miss Farraday. It is late. You are absolutely done in with fatigue. You will accept our hospitality for the night, and we will talk again in the morning."

"You are most kind, sir, but I cannot impose . . ."

"That, Miss Farraday, is bilge. Even if there were some way of getting you to town, you are far too tired to stand the trip. I apologize that we are not equipped for guests at Devon House; none of the spare rooms have been cleaned or aired in years." He sounded sad, as if the neglect of the house hurt him. "Anyway, I have ordered Chang to freshen my room for you. I think you will find it tolerable."

"I can't do that, not with your—your infirmity." It was bad taste to mention it, but there was no choice. "I can't turn you out of your own room. I'll make do with a couch or a pallet quite well."

For a moment something very soft and vulnerable flickered across his eyes, giving me a glimpse of what he must have looked like before his face became so gaunt and hag-ridden.

"You are very kind, Miss Farraday, but I assure you that, after being wrecked at sea and left for dead, a night spent on a comfortable camp bed will do me no harm."

"How horrible," I exclaimed and would have asked more about his adventures, but suddenly the ability to form words was beyond me. The revivifying effects of the brandy had been distressingly short-lived.

"Come. We must get you upstairs before you fall asleep on your feet. Climbing is a slow process for me."

My mind filled with questions, but my weariness had become an insurmountable barrier between me and rational thought.

At last the long sweep of stairs was negotiated, and Nicholas Berkley bade me a civil good night at the door of his—temporarily my—room. After the briefest of partings, I barely managed to strip off my soiled outer garments before falling into a sleep of exhaustion in a huge canopied bed carved with —what else?—dragons.

Chapter Four

I KNEW NOTHING save oblivion until an intrusive beam of sunlight lay full across my face and pulled me into reluctant consciousness. Still somewhat cushioned by the lassitude of awakening, I looked around the room. Except for the unusual bed, it was a very ordinary room, and though the filth was not as thick as in the library, it was evident that what cleaning had been done had been skimpy. What sort of household was this that possessed things of quality and richness only to allow them to sink under layers of grime and neglect?

Stretching, I changed position on the comfortable mattress, and my eyes took in the fantastic detail of the thick silk bed-curtains. I recalled the words of the odd little wagon driver.

"They be a queer people, the Berkleys," he had said during our lengthy drive. "Whole family's accursed, root and branch." At my exclamation that curses and such were just a bunch of nonsense, he had protested vociferously and told me their history, which indeed was most unusual and unlucky.

The house had been built in the last years of the previous century by Cecil Berkley, grandfather of the two men I had met the previous evening. Originally from New England, Cecil Berkley had gone to the islands to seek his fortune and, having married it, prudently brought both fortune and wife back to Connecticut after an abortive slave rebellion nearly cost him his life. His wife and her personal servant, who had been given to her at birth, both mourned for the islands and hated Berkley for bringing them to this cold, bleak land. Mrs. Berkley survived just long enough to give birth to a son. The slave woman said that the master killed her mistress by bringing her here, took the baby, and ran away. She was caught, of course, and just before she was hanged, uttered a dire and fateful curse against Berkley and all his family as long as they lived in this climate.

At first the curse was treated as a joke, but as the years passed, Cecil Berkley became odder and more reclusive. Finally, he hanged himself in what had been his wife's room. The boy, now a man and master of a ship built in his father's shipyard, sailed the profitable route between Macao and Singapore. Nelson Berkley was a man and master who knew no softness. He married Felicity Winterthorpe, a resident of the Singapore British Colony, to obtain British shipping licenses. When news reached him of Cecil Berkley's death, he took his bride home to the family mansion. Dismayed by the brooding pile, Felicity defiantly named it Devon House, after the almost forgotten green land where she had been born.

Finding both the tale and the setting a strain on my nerves, I had spent a great deal of time concentrating on other things rather than listening to the driver. Now I wished that I had paid greater attention. I had counted on Doro's sweet presence to make the place homelike; now it seemed that no one here had ever seen Doro.

With only a little reluctance, I pulled myself from the bed, a bit shocked to find that I had fallen asleep in my pantalettes and chemise. How Aunt Evelyn would berate such decadent and unladylike behavior! Despite my worry over Doro and the uncertain condition of my own future, the thought that I should never again have to worry over Aunt Evelyn and her dictums made me quite happy, a fleeting emotion quickly dispelled by a close inspection of what had been my best dress. There was no way it could be worn without a thorough refurbishing, and perhaps not even then. It would have to be the tartan, then, though it did not look nor fit well.

After my ablutions, I slipped into fresh pantalettes and chemise and tied on my new woven extension skirt which we had learned to wear instead of hoops. Eula had seen them in *Godey's Lady's Book* and would not rest until the sewing woman had made us some. An ingenious cage affair of graduated steel springs and taped weavings, it was lighter and cooler than the bulky crinolines, but at the moment I missed the added warmth of the old style.

As it became obvious that no servant was coming for me, and since I could find no bellpull to summon one, I set out to find my own way through the house. This proved easier than I had thought, for compared to the meandering complexity of Moonhaven, Devon House was comparatively simple—two wings flanked the central swirling stairway. The only remarkable thing about Devon House was its unbearable dirt. The hallways almost swam in dust and the air was thick and scented with an odd sweetish-sour odor that I could not name.

By daylight the hall appeared smaller and more beautiful than it had the night before. There was a purity of line and a quality of construction beneath the layers of dirt that appealed to me. I almost itched for an army of slaves to scrub, polish, and restore it to its rightful beauty before realizing that the North had no slaves. It certainly showed at Devon House; the slave quarters in Georgia were cleaner than this palatial house.

"It is a shame, isn't it?" Simon Berkley's voice cut across my thoughts. "I can remember when it fairly sparkled with polish and what appeared to be a million candles. Once my mother and father gave a ball; it seemed like the most exciting thing in the world. There were people here from up and down the coast, and Father had brought an orchestra all the way from Boston. I hid up there and watched." He indicated a spot at the top of the stairs.

"It seems such a dreadful waste," I murmured. I longed to ask what had brought such disaster, but managed to curb my tongue.

He shrugged. "One does what one can and must accommodate whatever situation exists," he murmured, then turned to me with a smile that was blinding with charm. "But you must forgive me, Miss Farraday! It is so seldom we have guests here that I forget my manners. Here I stand chattering like a monkey when you are undoubtedly wanting your breakfast! Come with me."

Indeed, the idea of breakfast—a real breakfast of eggs and beef and muffins—did sound wonderful after catching what food I could while traveling, but I hesitated to take his gaily extended arm. "Thank you, Mr. Berkley, but I really must see about getting back to Port Harmon and finding my cousin."

Another voice cut across the dusty air of the hall. "I admire your devotion to your family, Miss Farraday, but wherever Miss Conroe is, she will doubtless stay there until you finish your meal. I fear the dining room is quite impossible, so will you please come into the library?"

A flow of antagonism, as palpable as a cold stream, flowed between the two brothers. Simon's back grew stiff though his voice did not alter. "I thought we might have breakfast on the terrace, Nicholas. We'd best take advantage of the fair weather while it lasts."

Nicholas Berkley looked less supernatural by daylight, though he was still pale and drawn. In the glowing morning light, the livid slash on his cheek was dark and mottled, giving his cool smile a lopsided appearance.

"By all means, Simon. Take breakfast on the terrace if it pleases you. I require only Miss Farraday's presence to see if we can make some sort of sense out of this problem."

The younger Mr. Berkley was apparently used to his brother's manner, for he merely shrugged and said, "As you wish, Nicholas. I only thought our guest would prefer the fresh air to a stuffy library."

The library was indeed stuffy, though there was evidence that a hasty cleaning had taken place. The worst of the dust had been removed, and what remained had been rearranged sufficiently to make at least part of the room habitable. A low table was set with a beautiful assortment of china and silver, all showing the evidence of a quick cleaning. There were only two settings. Noting this, Simon nodded to the waiting and uneasy Chang, who disappeared and returned with another cover so quickly that he must have had it waiting just outside the door.

I watched the interplay of the three men with a slight curiosity, confirming my hazy suspicions of the night before. Nicholas might give the orders, but Simon was Chang's master. The opaque Oriental eyes never left the younger brother's face for long as if waiting for a countermand to Nicholas's orders.

Watching the actions of my hosts was certainly more interesting than eating their food. After one glance at what passed for breakfast, my hunger died. At Moonhaven, as at each of the Farraday homes where I had been raised, breakfast was all but a sacred institution, with hot breads and meats and jellies; here at Devon House it was a poor affair of plain boiled rice, greasy fish, and bread that resembled nothing I had ever seen. There was tea, though, and coffee so pungent it almost made up for the sad meal. I chose coffee, added milk, and tried desperately to think of my next move. Doro had to be somewhere.

"I apologize for the breakfast, Miss Farraday," said a smiling Simon. "Being two old bachelors more used to the deck of a ship than a house, we tend to let ourselves fall into slovenly ways. Besides, Chang isn't very much of a cook."

I choked down a bite of rice. "Is he your entire staff?"

"Some butter, Miss Farraday?" Nicholas extended the globe-like butter-keeper. It needed polishing. "Yes, Chang is all the help we have at the moment. I don't know why it has become impossible to keep servants at Devon House, but it seems that no one will work here."

"How very odd. Surely, with the influx of Irish and other laborers into your Eastern cities, there would be a shortage of jobs, not of workers." My tongue was again a bit hasty; I had been so occupied watching the incipient sparks between the two brothers that I had not given a thought to my words.

Simon started, but Nicholas only smiled lazily, and another dream of mine died. Apparently a thinking woman was just as much a freak in the North as in the South.

"You appear to be well-informed, Miss Farraday. I can only assume that you prefer your southern form of human bondage?"

"I was not aware of telling you that I came from the South, sir."

He poured more coffee. The hand on the pot was painfully thin. "It was not necessary, Miss Farraday. You betray your origins with every word."

"And a charming accent it is," Simon added.

Without a doubt, Nicholas Berkley was one of the most difficult men I had ever met; rather than give him the satisfaction of enlightening him about my home and family—which he was obviously waiting for me to do—I instead turned to his younger brother with a belle-like simper that even Cousin Flora would have envied.

"You are too kind, Mr. Farraday. I wanted to ask you—you said something about being more at home on a boat than here. Should I be addressing you as Captain or some other honorific?"

"In truth, Nicholas and I are both captains. One of us is always in command of our flagship, supervising the China trade. Berkley Limited is quite a big name in Singapore and Macao."

Such power and influence contrasted with the faded grandeur which surrounded me to such an extent confusion must have shown on my face. "But you're both here now?"

"Simon," his brother said ironically, "is trying to spare my feelings. I was bringing in the *Southern Cross* to spend my year at Devon House when the ship sank off the Sawtooth Reefs. So, he now has to wait until the second of the line, the *Evening Star*, comes into port in a few weeks."

"Then I shall go to the Singapore office for a year or so, while Nicholas holds the fort here, and then we shall change again."

"It seems a most unusual way to run a business," I murmured, pushing away my almost untouched plate.

Simon shrugged; his merry expression didn't change. "It is scrupulously fair; and we both learn both sides of the business."

"Are you finished, Miss Farraday?" Nicholas asked, and the slight change of his tone indicated the sociability of the breakfast hour was over. Indeed, as I nodded slightly, I thought I should feel most guilty for taking even that small amount of time away from the search for Cousin Doro.

After speaking in that queer tongue to the servant, Nicholas waited until Chang had cleared the table and left the room before turning his attention to me. Even with the drawbacks of his wound and the unkind morning light, he was a most commanding-looking man possessing a strength his brother did not show.

"Now, Miss Farraday, the question remains; what are we to do with you?"

I looked into his shadowed eyes and tried to restrain my sudden surge of annoyance. I had not come halfway across the country by myself to be treated like some kind of parcel!

"I think my next step is to return to Port Harmon and see what I can do to find my cousin Doro."

"Miss Farraday, I know very little about the southern culture, but I feel sure that they do not let gently bred young ladies of your tender years run about the country on their own. Does anyone know where you are?"

Beneath the mocking gaze of those fierce dark eyes, I suddenly felt unprotected and very vulnerable, as if he were looking at me without my shift. Then, to complete my humiliation, an awful blush arose, and all I could do was stare at my knotted fingers.

"I say, Nicholas! That's more than a little rude."

"Perhaps, but I dare say it's accurate. Since you are entirely on your own, Miss Farraday, do you intend to go on running about the country alone? Surely you have been told about the mysterious disappearances that have happened in this area?"

My face was aflame, but I met his gaze as calmly as possible. "That is all the more reason to reassure myself of my cousin's safety, sir."

"At the possible cost of your own?"

"Surely you do not believe that the Devil has come to earth to stalk about Connecticut!"

"Perhaps not the Prince of Evil himself, but surely some misbegotten soul with darkness in his heart. One can be killed just as surely by a man as by a demon," he said with so horrid a simplicity that I shuddered.

As if on a signal to complete that grisly moment, there came from the upper regions of the house a hideous cry, so chilling that my blood ceased to flow. The echoes of that inhuman sound hung in the still air even after the shrilling had at last died in a series of broken gurgles. For a moment I came close to believing the fantastic stories of the Evil One walking the land, for no human throat could have made that sound.

Even as the blood drained from my face and I almost shuddered with fear, my two hosts seemed unmoved by any emotion save annoyance. Nicholas heaved himself from his chair without the stiff hesitancy of a wounded man; perhaps the urgency in that banshee wail made him transcend his own infirmities.

With no warning, Simon grasped my cold hand in his two strong warm ones, his face thrust disconcertingly close to mine. He was indeed a most handsome man, despite the fact his chin was weaker than his brother's. The deep concern in his eyes, as they flicked from my face to the door through which Nicholas had just exited, more than made up for any such trifling defect in his physiognomy.

"I shall have to go, Miss Farraday, for he will be back in just a moment, but I beg of you listen to me. Get out of this house! You must not stay here one moment more than you have to. I'll drive you to Port Harmon myself, but you must get away from here!"

Chapter Five

AFTER UTTERING HIS urgent warning, Simon all but fled the room, just getting to the door as his brother testily called his name from the outer hall. The door slammed, and I was left alone with my chaotic thoughts. The atmosphere here at Devon House was unnerving enough without the twin horrors of the driver's tale and Simon Berkley's panicky warning.

Unable to be still a moment longer, I rose and paced the length of the room like a caged beast. It seemed that the carved, scaly creatures were only waiting until my back was turned to creep up on me in their silent stealth. Devon House, indeed! Dragon House would be more appropriate.

"My apologies," Nicholas murmured, shutting the door behind him. "I hope that our unfortunate incident didn't alarm you unduly."

"Indeed no, sir. Why should it alarm me that, in an area where the Devil is reputedly snatching young women, I hear a cry so horrible that it will doubtlessly echo in my dreams for months? Why should I be disturbed at all?"

Gingerly arranging himself in the high-backed desk chair, he smiled with a sweet kind of indulgence usually reserved for children. "You are frightened and small wonder, though I do admire your spirit. I make my apology to you yet again, Miss Farraday. Our mother is—not well in her mind." The admission was painful for him. The magnificent dark eyes clouded with strong emotion.

I looked away, trying to give him a moment of privacy for his grief. Bad enough that his mother was ill, but that her disorder was madness. . . . Apparently the old slave's curse on this household was still strong.

"I am sorry for you, sir. A sick parent is not an easy burden," I murmured in a spirit of kindness, remembering the sadness of Great-aunt Lorena's last months.

"I appreciate your sympathy, Miss Farraday, however," he said with surprising briskness, "that still leaves us the question of what we must do about you."

I looked at him with narrowed eyes. He was leaning back in the big chair, his brow furrowed in thought, as if the idea of anyone disagreeing with him had never entered his mind.

"Mr. Berkley, it is not necessary for you to do anything about me," I said haughtily. "I appreciate the night's lodging, and I would be most grateful if you would have me taken into Port Harmon. Beyond that you need not trouble yourself with me."

He smiled, and for one brief moment there was a glimmer of the vital man he must have been before the shipwreck. "Come now, Miss Farraday. I know you have no great love for us Northerners, but surely you see that I cannot let a gently bred young lady wander about the countryside as she pleases."

"And why not?"

"You do have spirit," he murmured admiringly. "Because, my innocent little miss, this is an evil world. If I were to cast you on the road as you desire, what would you do?"

How dare he be so patronizing when I had just proved my mettle by crossing the country alone? True, there had been some uncomfortable moments during my journey, but in the clash of battle I conveniently chose to forget them.

"Do, sir?"

"I know it's none of my business, but I should like to know." The wretch was smiling!

"I should try to find my cousin Doro, Mr. Berkley. That is why I came to this—" Several extremely unflattering words came to mind, but I suppressed them, "—part of the country. Should my inquiries in Port Harmon prove futile, I shall journey to Boston and speak to cousin Doro's aunt in person. If it becomes necessary I will apply to the police."

"You would expose your cousin's name in that fashion? The police do not enjoy a good reputation." His tone was almost teasing and I would swear that his eyes were smiling despite the solemnity of his face. "Might I offer you an alternative? You stay here at Devon House as my guest. Our company has very efficient men of business in both Port Harmon and Boston who can conduct thorough and discreet inquiries as to the whereabouts of your cousin."

"That is most kind of you, Mr. Berkley, but I must decline. Surely you can see that since you are a complete stranger to me I cannot cast myself on your mercy anymore than I have already."

Our eyes locked. The dusty, dragon-haunted room might not have existed as our wills struggled for supremacy.

"And surely you can see that I cannot allow a young woman such as yourself to walk away into what might be a dangerous situation. I must insist that you stay."

"Am I your prisoner then?" I asked slowly, my dreams sinking against the granite of his presence.

"My guest," Nicholas Berkley said. Although he smiled, it was a final declaration of the loss of my freedom. "Please, Miss Farraday, can't you understand that it would be most unchivalrous of me to do anything but return you to the protection of your family?"

I was so furious I could hardly speak. "I am not a parcel, sir!" I snapped fearlessly; the fear would come later, creeping like cold damp fog into the corners of my mind.

"No one suggested that you were," he said more gently than would have been expected, but I was too angry to notice. I babbled on in defiance, even as my inner mind was toying with the possibility of escape by stealth if necessary.

"As it is my intention to be an independent woman and look after myself, I cannot see where the conduct of my life affects either you or my family at all!" I pronounced with shaky dignity, miserably aware that it sounded far more like the spitting of a kitten than the declaration of a free woman.

To add to my fury, Nicholas Berkley laughed! "A blue-stocking, by God! Doubtless you want to vote, too?"

I saw no reason to dissemble in front of this odious man, and, although I had never really given the matter of suffrage a moment's thought, answered without hesitation. "Of course. I see no reason why a female cannot be just as informed as a man."

"Most revolutionary of you, Miss Farraday. I suppose you plan to obtain gainful employment to support yourself as well?"

I should have seen it coming; I should have seen what cunning traps lay beneath his honeyed words, but by now I was in too headlong a rush to heed any subtle warnings.

"Of course. I am strong and capable."

"What do you intend to do?"

This stopped me short as the wretch had probably intended, for although I had envisioned independence, I had never paused to see with what coin such freedom could be bought. I am totally unsuited for a governess, both from lack of patience and a disinterest in the babblings of very young children. I am very well versed in both economics and the field of classic literature, but my sex and the lack of a formal education would bar me from gainful employment in either field. My needlework is passable, as is my dressmaking, but beyond necessity such occupations do not appeal to me. The realization of my deficiencies was like a slap in the face.

"Why," he went on smoothly, covering my silence, "don't you accept the post of housekeeper here at Devon House? You can certainly see that we need one."

I argued, of course, as I had not yet learned that it was impossible to argue with Nicholas Berkley and win. We bickered back and forth until I was dizzy; the argument had passed beyond his summary assumption of my protection to something more basic, but all my rebuttals and pleas went unheard. I was stuck at Devon House until some way to escape could be devised. Simon Berkley's urgent warning still hissed in my ears, but now there was no way to heed it and escape this house of dragons.

"A housekeeper? How novel." Simon's words were bland, but his eyes spoke a different message to me. They were accusing, questioning, as if in some way I had hurt him. It made me extremely uncomfortable.

"I have agreed to lend the weight of Berkley Shipping to aid Miss

Farraday in her search for the elusive Miss Conroe. In the meantime, she will remain here at Devon House under my—our protection."

Again there were undercurrents, treacherous as any river-bottom quicksand, swirling in the dusty air. A strange tension existed between the two brothers, almost as if a line had been drawn between them defining their fields of honor. One could almost hear the rattle of sabers.

It was easy to compare the similarities and differences of the last two Berkleys standing face to face. Nicholas, though temporarily ailing from his recent tragedy, was whip-thin and hard in more than muscle; Simon was strong and handsome, but somehow unproven. When Nicholas completed his recuperation, he would be at least as handsome as his brother, but lacking Simon's appealing sweetness.

I shivered involuntarily. To be trapped in this accursed and eerie house with two strong-willed men and a madwoman . . .

Later as I walked the grounds it became obvious that I was indeed trapped. Devon House was all but a prison. The previous night I had been unable to see anything of the terrain including that which was right under my feet. Now I saw that Devon House was built on a rocky spit of land, surrounded on three sides by water. Only about twenty-five feet in height, the cliffs were sheer slices of rock, perpetually wet from the splashing breakers. Even today, when the sea was relatively calm, the rocks of the cliff face were shiny and slick with water thrown up from the jagged shards below. When the wind was high, the spray must come up level with the land.

I walked the perimeter of the cliff, watching the sea advance and retreat in a welter of hissing foam between the vicious rocks that edged the cliff bottom, and I recalled Nicholas Berkley's description of the Berkley property.

"It is a peninsula, thrust out of the sea and guarded by rough rocks below. At one time it was reputed to have been used by Colonial wreckers. They would light a beacon on the highest point of land, then when a ship, seeking a safe harbor, struck and broke apart on the rocks, the rogues would loot the wreck and probably kill the crew. When my grandfather acquired the place and built the house, he put a stop to such practices—if indeed they ever really did exist. Unfortunately, Grandfather was a great one for disagreeing with his neighbors, so he built a solid fence across the land neck to keep them out. You probably didn't notice it last night, but if the main gates are locked, no one can enter or leave Devon House."

Here he had stopped and smiled, as if trying to reassure me of my safety, but I found his smile and his story chilling. Ostensibly, he was trying to describe my temporary home, yet I could not help interpreting it as a warning, describing a prison rather than a haven.

I walked the perimeter again. This time I went more slowly, seeking any evidence of a path down the cliff or through the boulders that could be used as an escape route. There was nothing but rocks, wet, vertical, and cruelly broken. I could imagine too well a proud ship broken-backed on these rocks, dying slowly in the pounding surf while she was gutted by the scavengers.

My escape from Moonhaven had been the essence of simplicity compared to this place; I had merely chosen a time when no one would be around and walked out. There was a chilling thought: my escape from Moonhaven had brought me here. What hellish place could my escape from here bring?

I shuddered and looked upward to study the wheeling gulls. Despite the fact they were scavengers and garbage eaters, I thought their grey and white gracefulness lovely. How free their flight was.

Not so far in the distance the mainland sat, devoid of cliffs like the Berkley property, but fringed with jagged rocks every bit as vicious as the ones below me. There was a channel of deceptively calm water in between.

There was something below, a splash of vivid red and white cloth sticking from between the rocks not far below the top of the cliff. It was ridiculous, but my heart began to thud with painful intensity. A frightening intimation swept over me, draining my frame of strength. Luckily this was the furthest point from the house, and a slight undulation of the land hid me from all but the topmost floor, but it would have made no difference had I been directly in front of the main entrance. I had to have that piece of cloth!

By lying down fully on the coarse grass and leaning over the edge at a positively foolhardy angle, I managed to grasp the merest tip of the wind-whipped fabric and pulled it upward with the greatest of care, praying that no capricious breeze would snatch it from me only to deposit it in some utterly inaccessible place.

My care was rewarded. Soon I held the fluttering scrap in my hands. It had been a bertha, a popular combination of a shawl and a collar, made of white lawn and fancifully embroidered with red thread. I lifted the once-beautiful thing and tried to choke back my tears. This scrap of cloth held me to this somber place with restraints stronger than any Nicholas Berkley could devise.

This was Doro's bertha. I knew because not six months earlier I had made it with my own hands.

Chapter Six

I STOOD ON that rocky headland for some time, the bertha crushed in my insensitive grasp, looking unseeingly out at the restless ocean. *Doro had been here. Doro had been here!* That meant that she had been telling the truth, and that one or both of the Berkley men had been lying.

Unless there was a third Berkley brother . . . ? I had not seen evidence of anyone else, but that house could hold legions of people, and there was no direct evidence that this was the only home the family possessed.

I shook my head. Some inner instinct told me that the answer was here, and that all the players had been assembled. Over the generations men have made snide sport of woman's instinctual knowledge, but even in my insular world I had seen the truth of this gift often proved. Even that great realist, Great-aunt Lorena, had always advised me when in a situation requiring instant answers to trust my inner voices and good common sense. I had always admired Great-aunt Lorena as much as I had loved her and, after her death, had often longed for her counsel and advice. What would she have said to my present situation?

"Well, Drusilla my girl, you've gotten yourself into a pretty mess." I could almost hear her voice. Dear Great-aunt Lorena! How I missed her!

Resolutely, I turned my mind to the present problem of finding Doro. She had been here recently; of that I had proof. I was sorry to see that the red thread with which I had so carefully adorned the bertha had run with the wet—the pedlar had assured me it would not!—but it did give me a valuable piece of evidence; it had been placed here recently, elsewise the whole would have turned that inappropriately gay pink.

I knelt in the grass and looked over the edge. Some fifteen or twenty feet below were the wet grey rocks frosted with bubbling sea foam. There was no path that I could discern along that forbidding shore, nor any way down there; in fact, I could not see the cliff itself. It appeared to slope in as if undercut by the sea. The thought of it giving way and tumbling me into that rocky cauldron made me scramble hastily back from the edge. I have always been somewhat timid of high places.

Unless Doro had been taken away—for I could not believe she would hide of her own free will—she must be captive in the environs of Devon House. She had written to me of how she loved the bertha, a girlish overstatement perhaps, but there had been a ring of sincerity about her thanks. In any case, I could not see her tripping across the ground and lightly flinging it into the ocean! Not for the first time, I chastised myself for sleeping so sybaritically that morning; had I been awake, I might have seen Doro lose this.

But how could she lose it? How came this bertha to be here? I mean, a bertha is a fairly large article and, for decent women, somewhat indispensable. It covers the shoulders and fills in the bosom and is usually sewn or at least pinned to the dress itself, so that it can hardly be lost like a handkerchief or a cap.

Suddenly the wind off that grey, pitiless ocean was cold enough to cut to my bones. I entertained horrid visions of Doro, either bound or unconscious, being carried off like a sack of meal. The third alternative condition I could not bear to contemplate.

Did I dare share this piece of evidence with the Berkleys? I thought a moment, then finally decided not. I could not trust them; since I was now perforce installed in the house I did not need to reveal it. If they were guilty, what would stop them from taking the bertha away from me? If they were innocent, I could produce it later at the proper moment. No, for now this would be better kept as my private knowledge.

My own emotions were betraying me now. I felt anger and excitement coursing through my veins. There was fear, too, but only a small amount, hardly the equal of my challenging spirit. I vowed to rescue Doro, and the two of us would live a retired life together in peace and harmony.

As a good Christian woman, I have always believed in the triumph of good over evil, so I never doubted the inevitability of my success; however, my philosophy had never mentioned at what cost such triumph was to be achieved.

Unwittingly, Nicholas Berkley himself had given me the perfect entrée to fulfill my vow; as the housekeeper I would be completely free to search. There would be no part of the place into which I would not be able to pry. It was perfect.

The thought of housekeeping itself gave me few qualms; thanks to the excellent education given me by Great-aunt Lorena and the bits and snippets I had picked up from the various homes of my childhood, I had a fair idea of how to manage a household. I knew how to construct and adhere to a budget, how to set a table that was attractive and nourishing, and how to deal with slaves.

That, I conceded, might be a small problem. In the North they did not possess slaves, and I felt that handling strong-minded free servants would be a bit different than directing our own house people, most of whom had been born and raised at Moonhaven.

My fears appeared to be proven true at the first sight of the woman sitting stiffly upright in the library. After much thought, I had gone there to accept formally Nicholas Berkley's offer of employment. She was sitting erectly in the dragon chair I had occupied the night before, looking as outraged as she did alien.

"Ah, Miss Farraday," said Nicholas cordially, struggling to rise. Somehow the air of geniality sat uncomfortably on him, as a borrowed, ill-fitting garment. He looked as if he had not slept much, and I felt a rush of guilt for having ousted him from his own comfortable room. "Please come in and sit down. Mrs. Webber, this is Miss Farraday, who has bravely agreed to take on the Augean task of making Devon House liveable again."

The dreadful man! As if he had given me any choice in the matter!

Mrs. Webber was a stolid matron whose ample bulk radiated with disapproval as she gave me a curt nod that was just short of insolent.

The plumes on what was undoubtedly her best Sunday bonnet danced and jiggled.

"Mrs. Webber is the wife of our head stableman," Nicholas continued, waiting until I had perched on the edge of a chair before sitting down himself.

"I was not aware that Devon House possessed stables," I replied after a civil greeting to Mrs. Webber, once more speaking before I thought.

"Yes, we are not totally lacking in all the amenities." A wry smile played at the uninjured corner of his mouth. "Unfortunately the building must be outside the wall, as our little peninsula here is very small. You doubtless noticed that fact during your walk this morning."

I struggled to keep my face calm. So he had been watching me! And, my busy mind sped on, if the stables were outside the wall, the gates could not be kept locked the entire time and thus Devon House would not be as impregnable as Nicholas had intimated.

"Webber keeps the Devon House stables the best in the state. And Mrs. Webber is the best cook."

The worthy lady gave a snort that might have been learned from the most disdainful of her husband's charges and set her plumes jiggling again. "Now, Master Nicholas, don't you be trying to cozen me along like that. I've told you I'm not coming back to this place. It was only for courtesy's sake that I came when you asked this morning."

A cook! My spirits soared. How much easier my life would be if there were a cook here. I must admit that I was dreading the forthcoming meals, a situation very out of character for me. Aunt Evelyn had called my appreciation of food unladylike more than once.

"You were once the cook here?"

Mrs. Webber's round, flushed face turned to me. Her eyes were as pale and cold as sea stones. "Indeed I was. Cooked here from the week I married Webber in the summer of forty."

"And you won't come back?"

"I'll not stay where I'm called a thief," she huffed, a fire of righteous indignation heating her words. "If it were not for your poor dear mother, I'd not have stayed as long as I did, but when that heathen Chinee accused me—me˙that helped raise you and your brother both, Master Nicholas—of stealing and then your brother believed him—" Her words drowned in a gargle of anger.

"I cannot answer for what occurred in the house while Simon was in charge," Nicholas said smoothly. His face was white, the scar livid. I wondered if he were in pain. "I don't know what kind of a maggot got into Simon."

"Believing a Chinee—I vow I had nothing to do with it, Master Nicholas, but I'll not come back to this house! Not even if you were to fire Webber himself."

"There's no worry of that," Nicholas answered, and I realized then that he was tiring; if something were to be done to save the situation I should have to do it, for already Nicholas's mind was elsewhere, and Mrs. Webber was preparing to leave. I was bound to stay here until Doro was found, and I did not intend to stay on starvation rations!

"Exactly what was the charge, Mrs. Webber?"

She looked closely at me, and for a moment I was probed by her gaze. I was ruthlessly weighed and the balance must have swung in my favor, for she decided to answer civilly. Obviously she had been shocked at both my presence and appearance, but the cool voice of command—which I had borrowed from Aunt Evelyn—instinctually made her obey.

"That soft-footed, heathen Chang was always in and out of my kitchen, getting in my way while I was preparing the meals. Things began disappearing out of the larder. I complained to Master Simon, then that Chinee said I was taking them home. And Master Simon believed him!" Her bosom, tightly covered with good dowager purple, swelled with indignation.

"Without giving you a chance to defend yourself?"

"Defend myself? I was ordered out of the house!"

"Mrs. Webber," Nicholas began wearily, "again I cannot guess what Simon was thinking, but . . ."

"Such things," I snapped with a sudden fervor that surprised even

43

me, "will not be tolerated while I am housekeeper here. Mrs. Webber, I ask, no, I beg you to come back. Please." She was melting visibly, so I pressed my advantage. "Mr. Berkley is too much of a gentleman to mention it, but I will tell you I do not know how they have managed. The food here is dreadful; I doubt that Mr. Berkley would allow such to be served to the lowest seaman on any of his ships."

"I never thought . . ." she murmured.

"How can he be expected to recover his strength on a diet of ill-cooked rice and fish no cat would eat? As for the poor sick lady upstairs, heaven only knows on what she subsists!"

Startled, Mrs. Webber looked from Nicholas to me and back to him again. Her old loyalty was strong and her resistance weakening. As for Nicholas, he leaned back in his chair, his hand pressed to his lowered face. The only thing to spoil this picture of masculine need was that from my point of view I could see that the wretch was trying to stifle a laugh! How like a man indeed! I had spoken plainly, almost achieving what he himself had desired, and he was laughing at me for it. I was hard put not to empty the inkwell over his head.

"I had no idea things were as bad as that."

"Never lose your advantage," Great-aunt Pearl had told me. Of course, she had been talking of the hunting field, but the advice was apt here.

"Come, Mrs. Webber, let's go look at the kitchen and see what needs to be done to it." I stood and held out a coaxing hand.

Apparently, working with free servants was not going to be as different from working with house slaves as I had feared. Gentle authority seemed to work with both, for Mrs. Webber stood and began to strip off her gloves and bonnet. As we left the room, I heard a queer strangling sound.

Allowing Mrs. Webber the dignity of her domain, and concealing my ignorance of the house, I begged her to lead the way to the kitchen. It turned out I could have found my way there without difficulty, for as I have said before, Devon House was very simply designed compared to the labyrinthine complexity of Moonhaven.

The hallway we entered was narrow and dark and filled with a sour stench. As it ran between two rooms—the dining room and a butlers' pantry, I later learned—there were no windows and only one niggardly candle burning. It gave barely enough light to prevent us from walking into the dingy walls, and of what squeaked and scuttled in the darkness beneath our feet I preferred not to think.

One quick shove from Mrs. Webber's capable fist sent the door at the end of the hall swinging open to reveal a chamber only slightly less dark than the stygian hallway.

Mrs. Webber stopped dead on the doorstep. "Merciful heavens!"

Chapter Seven

IN THE DAYLIGHT the drive from Devon House to the gates was not
at all frightening, though the coming of day had not improved the
condition of the road. As Mrs. Webber and I walked it, skirting
pothole after pothole, I considered it a miracle that I had reached
Devon House as undamaged as I had! During the brief wait while an
astonished Mr. Webber hitched up a wagon, Mrs. Webber and I had
enjoyed a cup of tea. The kitchen, like everything else I could see of
the tiny house and more imposing stables, was spotless. Now I
understood why I had failed to see the place the night before; a
screen of brush shielded the buildings from the road. Doubtless the
Webbers went to bed early, and only a strong light could show
through that thick a hedge.

A taciturn woman by nature, Mrs. Webber did not rattle on as
the older ladies of my acquaintance invariably did; she spoke on
whatever subject was at hand, said what she intended to say and
then was quiet. I must admit it was restful.

On the other hand, it had been all the more surprising when,
after seeing the ruin of the kitchen, she had stalked angrily into the
library, berated a startled Nicholas for not telling her how low
things had sunk, and had announced that she and I were driving
into town that very day to see about hiring as many girls as it would
take to put the house aright. It was vastly amusing to see Mr.
Nicholas Berkley put in the same helpless position as he had put me.
No sooner had he given us his *carte blanche* than we were on the road
for Port Harmon.

Poor woman, it was easy to see that she was upset. The sight of
that kitchen had completely undone her. For that matter, knowing
that I had actually eaten food that had come from such a place

almost made me ill. It must have been horrible for Mrs. Webber, with her passion for cleanliness, to have seen the place she called her own for so long in such a state.

Great piles of refuse had littered the shadowed floor; dishes from many meals past stood stacked on the counters, some veiled by spiderwebs. The nauseous smell of decomposing food assailed our nostrils and one of the top plates rocked ominously as a rat, disturbed at his dinner, scampered away.

Even now in the bright noon sunlight and the brisk wind, the memory of that disaster made me shiver.

"Cold?" asked Mrs. Webber.

"A little." I huddled in my cloak and tried to keep my teeth from chattering. Somehow I had never realized how cold cold could be.

"You need to get some warmer clothes. You'll never survive winter with those."

Winter? Even though this was September and the harsh winter of this land not far away, I had never considered staying through it. Somehow I would find Doro and—my inventiveness failed.

Port Harmon was not much more impressive by day than it had seemed by night. Small and dingy, it was somehow unwelcoming and closed in upon itself. Was this the town where Doro had grown up with such enjoyment? Had I actually envied her life here? Somehow I had pictured her skating parties and entertainments as taking place in a much more exciting setting than this!

"Come," said Mrs. Webber as soon as she stopped the wagon and, after clambering down, tied the horses to a post. "First we'll order the supplies and ask Fred Jenkins if he knows of any girls to hire."

I meekly followed her into the clapboard building. Only a sedate sign proclaimed that it was a store: there was none of the clutter of brooms and churns and buckets about the door as there would have been back home.

Inside it was like no other store I had ever seen. There were the bolts of yard goods, yes, and the jars of penny candy and the shining new tinware; on the other wall, however, were ship's lights and stacks of canvas and rope and great mechanical things whose use I could only guess. A faint acrid aroma of tar vied with the tang of the pickle barrel and the sweet sawdust on the floor, making a queer scent that I found myself liking.

"Good afternoon to you, Mrs. Webber," said the man behind the counter. Spare and sad, he reminded me of a more articulate version of the Reverend Mr. Entwhistle. I was happy to inspect the contents of the store and allow Mrs. Webber to handle the negotiations.

"Good morning, Mr. Jenkins. That young lady is Miss Farraday, the new housekeeper at Devon House. We are here to purchase supplies." The steely glint in her eye discouraged any gossip, but human curiosity is a powerful thing.

"Are you back at the Berkleys' then?" Mr. Jenkins asked mildly, reaching for a pad and a stub of a pencil.

"Yes," she replied shortly, then began dictating a list of incredible length.

Not wishing to interfere, I wandered over to the yard goods section. What Mrs. Webber had said about clothes made me think perhaps I could use another dress; after all, I only had two, and one of them was nearly ruined. I didn't feel my needlework up to the construction of a dress, but if there were a sewing woman in the town . . .

A length of scarlet wool caught my eye. Stepping to the window, I examined it with pleasure. The jewel-like color was the first bright thing I had seen in this drab country. It was indeed beautiful, but sadly it would never do for me. Reluctantly I put it back on the counter and turned my attention to a bolt of dreary but serviceable brown alpaca.

"You're back!" a feminine voice shrilled in my ear. "Where have you been? We've all been so worried." Strong hands whirled me around to face a young woman who blanched at the sight of me.

By now I was becoming accustomed to rudeness, so I merely stood and looked at her. I hesitate to admit even now that I failed to see the significance of her astonishment, putting it down as yet another black mark against Yankee manners. Truly, I should be ashamed of such blind prejudice; my only defense is youth, fatigue, and an almost criminal stupidity.

"Please forgive me," she stammered, blushing to the roots of her hair. Young and well-dressed, she was obviously embarrassed at having made a mistake common to all of us—that of taking one person for another.

Perhaps I should have figured it out then; I like to think that I would have, had not Mrs. Webber called to me. Her acceptance of me was a puzzle, too. Surely things could not be so different in the North that she would receive a young lady of my station in my position with equanimity, but apparently she had. Either she was an extremely charitable and broadminded woman or Nicholas Berkley carried a great deal of weight with her. I was inclined to think the latter.

"Our order will be loaded by the time we come back."

"Back?"

"Mr. Jenkins says that there are a number of young persons desiring employment in town."

Delighted to have my opinions vindicated as to the availability of labor in this area, I nodded. "I thought as much. Immigrants?"

"Not many. Mostly local girls come in to work at the mill at Cooperville." Correctly, she allowed me to precede her out of the door. "More want to work than the mill can take. Seems they find work in a town mill more attractive than staying home on the farm."

I was shocked. At home, no one but the poorest kind of white trash allowed their womenfolk to work in the fields and to do so was to admit complete loss of status. More kindly than I deserved, Mrs. Webber informed me of certain facts of northern life. I listened intently, trying to learn as much of these strange people as I could, until a whining voice rasped its way into my consciousness.

". . . all in black, she was, and veiled all over like she was wearing a shroud. Spoke like a Christian, she did, but I knew she was the Devil's handmaiden as soon as she asked to go to Devon House. . . ."

It was my driver! Even more unprepossessing in daylight, he sat at ease in his dilapidated wagon for all the world as if holding court. Clustered around him were a group of drifters and loafers, all hanging on his every word with undisguised skepticism; it seems every town, North and South, has its share of these ne'er-do-wells.

"Ah, give over, Abijah! Weren't ye afeered?" scoffed a rough-looking fellow in a red cap.

The driver favored them with a disdainful look. "Happen not. I'm a good Christian."

"Besides," laughed another coarsely, "the Devil is only interested in young girls."

An older man, his vacant look an indication of his greater credibility, stared up worshipfully. "What happened then, Abijah?"

"Happen I took her out to Devon House and let her down. And the darkness just swallowed her up! Disappeared like she wasn't ever there! Reckon the Devil claimed his own, I do!" Basking in the glow of his cronies' admiration, the little man sat back like a conquering hero. It was more than I could stand.

"That he didn't was no fault of yours! Leaving a lone woman out in the dark without even the courtesy of taking her to the door of her destination!" I snapped, shaking an admonitory finger at him. "And the only way I could get you to go as far as the gates was to pay you a disgracefully high fee. You should be ashamed of yourself for such ungentlemanly practices instead of bragging about them!"

Stung, the little carrier started forward. The reaction among his audience was equally cowardly; all of them stepped back a pace or two and one—the vacant faced half-wit—broke into a shambling run.

"And you," I added angrily to the onlookers, my memory of that awful walk still painfully fresh, "all of you should be ashamed of yourselves for listening to this man brag about his uncharitable conduct!"

"Just like the other one," one of them breathed.

"The Devil's mark . . ."

The driver raised a shaking finger. "Red hair. She has red hair, too!"

Suddenly I knew and wondered why I had not known before. Self-description had held little place in the course of Doro and my letters, since vanity is a cardinal sin, and I had been so ashamed of how apart from the rest of the family my "different" hair color set me. My mother's hair.

"Dorothea Conroe was a redhead," I murmured.

"Happen so," the driver answered. For all his self-vaunted courage he looked very uncomfortable, as if I were some spectre risen to haunt him.

Doro was a redhead! Of course, our mothers had been sisters, and red hair tends to run in families. Unfortunately, I continued in my stupidity, and the thought died there. The Good Book says that to seek revenge is wrong and that pride is a sin; I was in the full throes of both, for my main thought was of chastising the cringing little man instead of concentrating on the matter of Doro's disappearance—a mistake for which I would pay dearly.

"I cannot believe it is the custom of all northern drivers to extort ridiculous fees from a lone woman and then leave her stranded in the wilderness in deference to their own cowardice!" I said in tones loud enough to reach across the cobbled street. By now I was in a fine welter of emotion. Redheads are reputed to have tempers, and Aunt Evelyn always said that I was walking proof of it. "But then to extol their Christian virtues . . ."

"Miss Farraday!"

The cultured voice cut across my heated tones, and I looked up, blushing quite as red as my unfortunate hair. Recalled too late to a sense of proper behavior, I could scarce meet the eyes of Mr. Simon Berkley. Last night I had appeared an unmannerly waif, and today I appeared a Xanthippe, little better than a common shrew; perhaps it was something in this brisk northern air which made everyone appear less than their best.

"My dear girl, what on earth are you doing here?" He dismounted gracefully from a blooded horse that looked to be mostly of the fabled Arabian strain.

"This is the creature who abandoned me at your gate last night," I cried with righteous wrath, pointing an accusing finger at the cringing man.

"If you had the ill fortune to get into this rickety thing," he said with a laugh and kicked the wheel of the old wagon; it shuddered as if it too were afraid. "I'm surprised that you got as far as you did. Abijah, you old scoundrel, you better get out of here before you get the treatment you deserve."

Abijah did not need to be told twice. He slapped the reins across his horse's back with such unaccustomed vigor that the poor old nag was startled into a faster pace than he had achieved in many a day.

"Maybe he will be a bit more accommodating to his passengers now," I said pettishly. I had a great many more things that I wished to say to that wizened creature and felt cheated of the right.

"I doubt it. Old Abijah is one of the town characters. He'll never change. I'm only sorry that you had to encounter him your first day in Port Harmon. Please don't let him affect your opinion of the rest of us." Taking another step closer he smiled in such a way that it would have taken a stronger female than I not to feel a flutter of admiration.

"Miss Farraday!"

Apparently Mrs. Webber was just such a female; her voice fell around us like a bucket of freezing water. She was still standing on the granite walk, and her expression was only slightly less hard. She looked at Simon with an expression of concentrated loathing.

The light in Simon's eyes died, replaced by a curiously guarded expression. "Mrs. Webber," he said with cold courtesy, doffing his hat just enough to remain in the sphere of politeness.

The cook ignored him. The only sign that she could see him at all was that her mouth thinned down to a compressed line of disapproval. "If you are going to be much longer, Miss Farraday, might I suggest that I go speak to the minister about some suitable girls?"

It was as good a solution as any. Although I ran the risk of incurring her displeasure, it was much more important to me to talk with Simon and perhaps increase my knowledge of the mystery surrounding Doro's whereabouts.

"Perhaps that would be best, Mrs. Webber. Suppose I meet you here in an hour?"

Her expression was distressingly eloquent, but without comment she gave the barest of nods and moved down the street like a ship in full sail. I was afraid it would take a great deal to get back in her good graces again.

Simon's face darkened. "I'm not happy to see you with that old besom."

"Mrs. Webber? She said there were bad feelings between you two."

"I am not in the habit of maintaining cordial relations with thieves," he said shortly. "Will you walk with me?" Taking my acquiescence for granted he draped my arm through his, and we started down the street.

As I have stated before, Port Harmon was an unprepossessing town, especially when compared to the bustling port of Savannah. Our steps took us toward the wharves—nearly every street ended there eventually—and although there were a very few ships in, I thought it much more eye-catching than Savannah, the only other port of my experience.

"Do you really think Mrs. Webber is a thief?" I was not through with the question.

"Would you care to sit here?" With consummate courtesy, Simon gestured to a bench. It was actually on the wharf itself and unshielded from the ocean breeze. Once more I was reminded of my cloak's inadequacy. All in all, though, it was not too unpleasant, for the breeze carried away the noxious odors endemic to any port, though in all honesty I must admit they were milder here than the stench which marked Savannah harbor.

I arranged my cloak, trying to knock off the sharpest of the wind while Simon tied his horse. "Are you avoiding my question, Mr. Berkley?"

"About Mrs. Webber? No, I believe she is a thief, and I am not happy to see you hand in glove with her. I suppose this means you are taking Nicholas's moonshine about being a housekeeper seriously."

"Of course I am. You certainly can't deny you need one!" I replied with some asperity, the memory of that hideously filthy kitchen still fresh in my mind. If by some chance such a place had existed at Moonhaven, Aunt Evelyn would have ordered it burnt.

"I don't deny it," he said with feeling. "You forget I have had to live in that mess, thanks to dear Mrs. Webber!"

"Mrs. Webber! Surely you can't mean she . . ."

"No, it was clean enough while she was there, but since I dismissed her, she has made sure that no one else will work at Devon

House. The vicious old gossip probably blamed us for everything but the bad catch this year!"

"Then why would she come back?"

"Probably because Nicholas asked her. She was always dotty about him." A ghost of childhood jealousy was evident in his voice. "She'd come back just to make me out a liar."

"Are you so certain of her guilt?"

He looked beyond me to the sea. His eyes were brown, like his brother's, but where Nicholas's eyes were a dark, smoky color, Simon's were lighter and golden, like old honey. "She has certainly done a job on you, hasn't she?" His voice was harsh.

"I have heard her version of the story, but now I should like to hear yours."

He studied me for a moment, then, surprisingly said, "Dear Miss Farraday, you shouldn't let yourself be dragged into our quarrels. This is no place for you. Let me help you . . ."

"Mr. Berkley . . ."

"You're a lady, not a housekeeper!"

"I must earn my keep, Mr. Berkley. Even ladies must eat."

"Surely you have a family somewhere. Let me help you return to them."

I had no intention of doing so, of course, but for one moment a vision of returning to Moonhaven did appear to me. Aunt Evelyn would be furious, Flora and Eula would be catty, and Uncle Richard would harrumph noisily before seeking refuge in the billiard room. No, even the thought of going back to Moonhaven was distasteful, and it must have shown on my face, for Simon forgot himself and gripped my hands.

"No, I see that will not do. Then let me help you build a new life, Miss Farraday. I can help you until you get a new position, a good position away from us and our problems." His voice flowed with sincerity. I believe I could happily have taken his aid had Doro not been involved, but then, if it wasn't for Doro, I should not have been mixed up in the Berkleys' affairs anyway!

"You are most kind, Mr. Berkley, but I cannot accept your help."

He shrugged and stared out to sea, his eyes gone dull. I

disengaged my hands from his grasp and folded them in the warmth of my cloak. Indeed, if I did intend to spend much time in the out-of-doors, I should need warmer clothing!

After a moment's silence, I asked him again for his version of the difficulty with Mrs. Webber. He answered in a bored voice, telling me approximately the same story as Mrs. Webber had, except he cast himself as the hero instead of the villain.

". . . and now she blackens our name before the world," he concluded at last, and it was as if the sun came out when he suddenly smiled. Simon Berkley did have the most enchanting smile!

"But she has come back to work for you."

"She has come back to work for Nicholas, probably to defend her reputation or to gain more spoils for herself."

"I thought there was nothing but food missing."

"So far as we know. Webber makes good money; I don't know why she steals."

"Is there any chance of the Oriental . . . ?"

He looked startled. "Chang? You think Chang might be the thief?"

"He was there, wasn't he?"

"My dear Miss Farraday, Chang has been with us since he was a child. He was raised at Devon House. His mother has been my mother's servant since she married my father. They are almost family!" Dismissing the matter, he cast a knowing glance at the sky. It was grey with lowering clouds; the wind was picking up, sending them scurrying inland as if for shelter.

"If you're so intent on this lunacy, I'd better get you and Mrs. Webber on your way back to the house," he said suddenly, standing up and pulling me with him. "There's a goodish blow coming up."

"Do you think we'll be caught in it?" It was foolish, I knew, but I disliked storms. All that noise and flashing light . . . I never quite committed the cowardice of hiding my head in a pillow like Flora, but during the most violent thunderstorms I was most likely to be found reading, my face resolutely to the wall. Apparently Simon's charger shared my opinion, for he began to dance nervously.

"Not if you leave quickly enough. Come, I'll even help you find Mrs. Webber."

It was a generous offer, but as we climbed up the cobbled street back to the commercial area I began to be recalled to my sense of purpose. I had not come to New England to be a housekeeper; my mission here was to find Doro, and the problems of the Berkley brothers were none of mine! I wished I had had the foresight to bring Doro's letters with me.

"Do you know," I asked, taking Simon's proferred arm over a particularly rough stretch of pavement, "if there is a circulating library in town?" Perhaps there someone could give me some information on Doro; she and her Mr. Berkley had met there. Surely someone would remember!

"A library?" he asked after a moment. "I suppose so, but you will have to ask Nicholas. He's the bookish one in the family. If you like to read, I'm sure he won't mind you using the library at Devon House. There are enough books there, in truth."

I remembered the library, with its books undisturbed under a blanket of dust. "True, but hardly current."

Mrs. Webber had completed her task quickly. She sat ramrod straight in the wagon seat, and behind her, disposed as best they could on the assorted barrels and bales of supplies, were three healthy-looking young women. Apparently they had been chosen more for their sturdy arms than for their slightly stupid expressions.

It was an uncomfortable situation, with the atmosphere between Mrs. Webber and Simon Berkley being no less electric than the storm growing over our heads. Everyone behaved with great civility as Simon and I were introduced to Alice, Charity, and Maud, but I held my breath lest an unwary word set fire to the palpable antagonism. All in all, as much as I enjoyed Simon's company, it was a relief when he mounted his noble steed and, pleading business that would not wait, rode away to the south.

Chapter Eight

OUR ROAD LAY to the north. I watched the lowering clouds, afraid that they seemed to be darkest right where we were heading. It seemed somewhat appropriate; Devon House was more a structure of night and storm than of light and sunshine, not that any appreciable sun had shone this day.

"We were fortunate," Mrs. Webber was saying. "The parson said several young persons had sought shelter with him after the mill turned them down. I really don't know what he'll do with the rest of them."

Mrs. Webber had just turned the horses from the highroad onto the lane when the left horse shied and reared as high as his harnesses would allow. He set off down the road at a gallop, perforce taking the rest of us with him. Panic is contagious, and before we had covered ten yards the other horse was running as fast as his mate in equal fear.

Whatever else her qualifications for driving, Mrs. Webber was not equal to panic. The reins slipped uselessly through her fingers until she recalled her duty, but by then the horses had their bits in their teeth and would not respond.

We swayed wildly in the careening wagon as it bounced over the rutted road. The trees alongside us swept by madly until it seemed that we could not be going that fast, that the trees had to be running the other way. Perhaps it was the thought of trees running that broke my shocked stupor, or perhaps it was the shrill screams of the three girls, who somehow contrived to sound like many more, but I suddenly realized that we were all in a fair way to being killed unless something was done that minute.

I am not overly proud of my action. It is wrong to cause distress to a dumb animal, but I must admit that thought didn't enter my mind until later. Bracing myself strongly against the fascia board, I wrenched the reins from Mrs. Webber's frozen fingers and jerked them with all my strength. Uncle Richard would have had a spasm, for he says that a horse's mouth is their most sensitive part and that if it is hardened or injured, the animal might as well be destroyed. That's as may be, but I will put my life up against a horse's mouth any day.

The struggle seemed to last forever, yet it could not have been more than a few seconds before I began to triumph, and the wagon slowed down. A few seconds more and the animals were stopped, their sides heaving like bellows and with great gobbets of foam dripping from their mouths. The girls behind us continued to shriek and moan until I snapped, "Be quiet! You don't want to set them off again!" and blessed silence descended.

"Well, I wonder what made them start like that?" Mrs. Webber asked. To her credit she neither shrieked nor swooned, and her quiet good sense calmed the rest of us. "They've never bolted before in their lives."

Indeed the poor beasts seemed to be glad to quit running, and the rest of our progress to Devon House was as sedate as we could have wished. I thought no more of the incident until later, when Mrs. Webber told me that while examining the beasts her husband had found a great bruise on the rump of the left horse as if it had been hit by an energetically thrown stone.

The rest of the ride back we assuaged our battered nerves by making plans. We discussed a great number of schemes but finally decided that the girls would try to make headway in the kitchen first, as least enough to prepare a decent meal. That would also occupy them while I took advantage of my status to search the house alone. Surely if Doro had ever been here I would find more than just a sea-stained bertha!

Webber was just putting away a large bay hunter—more impressive, if possible, than Simon's roan—as we drove into the yard. He greeted the girls with pleasure, then exclaimed in horror as we told him of the horses bolting. The small, wiry man always seemed inarticulate in conversations with human beings and more at ease talking to horses; from that moment he was lost to us as he crooned nonsense words to the horses while he examined them for any injury. As far as he was concerned we had ceased to exist. It was dreadfully lowering.

"May I speak to you, Mr. Berkley?"

He looked up from the library desk. For a man immersed in thick and dusty ledgers, he looked suspiciously pink-cheeked and healthy. Even the scar on his cheek appeared less raw.

"Of course, Miss Farraday." He struggled to a standing position, wincing as he did so, and motioned me towards the sinister-looking dragon chair. "Please sit down."

"Thank you, sir."

He eased himself back into his own chair. "I'm surprised to see you back so early."

"We hurried. It looks like it is going to storm."

"Yes, the glass has been falling since not long after you left. I considered coming after you."

Of course. The horse had to have been his. "Are you sure riding is beneficial for your condition?"

He smiled, and once more that magical transformation took place, giving his face light and warmth. "I see my secret is out."

"Webber was stabling your horse just as we arrived."

"Timing has always been one of my weak points." He didn't even bother to look shame-faced. "No, Miss Farraday, riding is definitely not beneficial for my condition, as you so delicately put it, and Dr. Debenham would doubtless give me the devil—begging your pardon—if he knew I had gone out."

Men!

"Then why did you do it? To do an act that is obviously deleterious to your health—"

Perhaps sensing a lecture, Nicholas held up a languid hand. "Because, my inquisitive Miss Farraday, I wish to prove, to myself if no one else, that I am not yet a vegetable. A long term of inactivity has an even more deleterious effect on a man than a short ride.

Besides, I didn't go far. Now, that is enough of my iniquities; tell me of your successes."

"My successes, sir?"

"Can it be anything less? You did obtain supplies and maids and whatever else you needed, didn't you?"

He was teasing me, so it only seemed fair . . .

"I found nothing, sir," I answered meekly and had the satisfaction of seeing him jump.

"You surprise me, Miss Farraday."

"We did procure both maids and supplies, but it was all the doing of Mrs. Webber. I accomplished little." Actually I had accomplished a fair amount, but none of it in the fields which would interest him. "However, I fear there is a little problem. I must oust you from your room for one more night."

He shrugged the problem away. "It is of no importance. You did obtain help, though?"

I told him of the mill's over-popularity and Mrs. Webber's ease in obtaining what she called suitable girls, and the great amount of supplies she had ordered, and the plans we had made. I did not tell him anything else.

He sat and stared at me for one of the longest moments of my life, as if willing me to say more. I returned his gaze as calmly as I could. Finally, he assumed a cloak of heartiness and said, "So I suppose that means we will have a decent meal tonight."

"Yes, sir. Mrs. Webber promised me that she would contrive something."

"Did you happen to see Simon in town? He said he was riding that way."

Obviously he knew the answer as well as I. Great-aunt Lorena had once said that the thought processes of most males were lamentably simple; she had also said that the best way to confound some people was to tell the truth.

"Yes, as a matter of fact, I did. He and Mrs. Webber really don't get along, do they? Mr. Berkley was so kind as to talk to me while Mrs. Webber interviewed the girls." I hesitated, then added, "He asked me if I were truly taking this nonsense of being a housekeeper seriously."

"And are you?"

"I told him I must earn my bread." I hoped he would not demand to know more of my meeting with Simon, for now that my temper had cooled I didn't care to spread the story of my disgraceful behavior with the driver any further than necessary.

"While you search for your cousin."

"While I search for my cousin." I struggled to maintain my composure under his scrutiny.

"You possess a strength of resolution not usually found in females. In one so young it is truly remarkable. Perhaps there is some facet of southern upbringing which we should investigate more carefully."

Echoes of Aunt Evelyn's lectures rang in my head. "I am hardly a pattern card, sir. Now, may we discuss my duties?"

"You are a glutton for punishment, Miss Farraday. Surely you have done enough for today." His dark eyes locked with mine and I thought I saw a glitter of humor in their smoky depths although his face was stern.

"Soonest started, soonest finished," I replied evenly. "I should like to see the house."

"So you can start looking for your cousin? Do you really think we keep her locked up in a cupboard?" he asked easily, giving me more than a little start. I had not known I was so transparent.

"Do you?" I replied, hoping that I looked a great deal calmer than I felt.

"It would be so much simpler if you would take my assurance that she is not in the house. Then we could play a game of chess before dinner."

"Chess, Mr. Berkley?"

"You do play, don't you?"

Of course I played. Great-uncle Edgar, Great-aunt Pearl's husband, had been crippled in a riding accident, and it had fallen my lot to amuse him. There is very little common ground for a child of eight and an elderly man, but Great-uncle Edgar did teach me chess, and we played until his death. Since then I had had little opportunity to practice, but chess learned well is never really forgotten.

"A little."

"I thought you would."

Perhaps I had never been more than a poor relation and expected to amuse my betters, but I had never known it showed! Stung by his calm assumption of my status, I pulled myself erect and demanded, "And what made you think that, sir?"

The wretch completely undid me with his reply. "Because most intelligent people do. And don't try any southern belle tricks about it. I'll expect you to play to win."

"I never play any other way!" I snapped, then forced myself to draw a deep breath. He was trying to bait me, and I would not let myself be drawn!

"No," he murmured, "I didn't think so. Did you find out everything you needed to know in town today?"

He was trying to take me off guard with his double-edged question; I returned his steady gaze as calmly as I could. "Not everything. Do you happen to know if there is a lending library in Port Harmon?"

At least I had surprised him! His brows knit. "I believe so. My mother used to have a subscription there, before—I'm sure it would be easy to procure another if—"

"No, thank you, not right now. I'll have too much to do here."

"Looking for your cousin."

"Yes."

"She really isn't here, you know."

It would have been so easy to believe him. But . . . I myself had found Doro's bertha not a hundred yards from where we sat; if she were not here, where was she?

"Perhaps not," I said carefully, "but dust and dirt certainly are. May I go?"

He shrugged. "If my captains had only half your tenacity, Miss Farraday, Berkley and Sons would be a much wealthier company. Come." He struggled to his feet.

"Please, Mr. Berkley!" I cried, truly alarmed at how strained his face became. He had obviously overdone himself today; besides, I wanted no guided tour nor overseer while I searched for Doro. Since he was being so open, I doubted that she was in the house proper, but I could not afford to be complacent. "There's no need. I can see everything myself."

"I've not the slightest doubt of that," he said, his features slowly returning to normal. "However, I'd best introduce you to Yu-Wei before she puts a dagger through you."

The casual mention of such violence gave me a start. "Yu-Wei?"

"Chang's mother. She's been my mother's attendant for years."

"Of course. Your brother mentioned her just this afternoon. I had forgotten."

Nicholas made no reply to that; instead he seemed to be concentrating his energies on climbing the stairs, leaning heavily on his cane. In the interest of his health, I remonstrated with him again for riding when his injuries were so obviously unhealed, and for my concern I received only a curt instruction to mind my own business. It set a stiffness between us that did not break until we were in the upper hallway.

The strange odor that I had noticed before was faint here, but it grew stronger as we turned down the opposite hallway from where I had slept.

This wing was different from the other; in place of the window at the end of the hallway, there were heavy double doors. Two lamps, long uncleaned, hung from brackets and gave only scanty illumination. Even in that uncertain light, I could see—and was not the least surprised—that the doors were covered with two enormous, entertwined dragons; in the flickering lamplight they almost appeared to be writhing. The sweetish odor grew heavier, and my stomach started to churn.

One door opened at Nicholas's first knock; the dragon carving swung back, sending waves of that sickly-sweet stench flooding over us. Manners forced me to drop the handkerchief I had pressed to my nose, but I wondered if I could hold my uncertain stomach still.

Beyond the door there was only a dim light, one that made the hallway appear bright by comparison, and a rolling cloud of smoke that for a moment made me think of fire.

"There has been no noise," said a voice in soft, birdlike tones. It spoke in an easy and almost childlike manner, but still the hairs on the back of my neck tensed. A tiny creature clad in trousers stepped out of the roiling gloom, and it took a moment before I realized it was female. If I had ever known Chinese women wore trousers, I had forgotten it; for a moment I was lost in mingled astonishment and envy—amazement that she should be so brazen as to continue such an immodest custom on our shores and envy for her costume seemed to offer so much more mobility and comfort than our bulky hoops and skirts.

"I know, Yu-Wei. You have done well today," Nicholas said with grave formality. "I merely wish to introduce our new housekeeper, Miss Farraday. You will be seeing her—"

And now I could see her, see the oval of her face, framed by a smooth helmet of black hair sleeked back into a simple knot. Her almond shaped eyes, set deeply into an ageless face, narrowed to vicious slits. "She will not disturb Missee! She will not set foot in these rooms."

"Don't worry," Nicholas said in a queerly tight voice. "I would not ask her to. But, she has my permission to go anywhere else she wishes."

"Not Missee's rooms, ever!" the old Chinese woman snapped.

She was about to say more, but a thin voice, reedy and piercing, floated out of the gloom. "Who is that, Yu-Wei? Do we have visitors? Is it one of my boys?" In the shadows of roiling smoke, I saw a small, hunched figure moving toward us with outreached hands. It was an image from a nursery nightmare.

A look of acute distaste flashed over Nicholas's face, and he made a quick, automatic gesture of negation. As one who had lived her life without knowing a mother's love, in that moment I hated him for his rejection of her in her illness.

"It is nothing, Missee," Yu-Wei called. "She does not come in here," she hissed, glaring at me as she soundlessly closed the door.

Nicholas's face was set and rigid. He gave me the slightest of bows, saying, "The freedom of the house is yours," then limped away as if afraid of contamination.

I followed, more slowly, my knees shaking with every step I took. There was a small bench at the head of the stairs. I sank down onto it gratefully. Never had I had a more uncomfortable encounter, not even with Aunt Evelyn at her worst.

After a moment of calm, which I spent praying for strength and courage, my head began to clear. I hadn't quite reached the point of wishing I had never left Moonhaven, but I did think pensively of my original dream of finding shelter with a loving, welcoming Doro.

My back erect enough even to satisfy Great-aunt Lorena, I walked to the far end of the hall and looked out the window. I knew it could be no later than mid-afternoon, but the sky was as dark as dusk. I could hear the moaning of the wind, soughing around the corners of the house like a sick animal. It was a very lonely sound. The clouds above me were dark, low, and angry-looking, and I felt sorry for anyone who was outside even though the rain had not yet begun to fall.

Cautiously taking a lamp, I began looking behind doors. At one time these had been princely rooms, decorated with good furniture and fine things. The furniture was still in place, probably just where it had been when the house was built; there were almost no bibelots, which I assumed had been packed away, though the carpets and hangings had been left in place. Everything was now sadly neglected, though none of the rooms were in as bad a shape as I had expected. What a showplace this must have been in its prime!

The only two fully habitable suites I found belonged to the two brothers. Nicholas's chambers were much more elaborate with dragon-covered furnishings. Simon's suite was just as impressive in its way; an imposing antique four-poster bed filled most of the room, dwarfing everything else. It was also by far the cleanest. Through an open door I could see the dressing room and a corner of the camp bed on which Nicholas slept. It looked none too comfortable and I vowed that tomorrow night there would be a room ready for me so that he could reclaim his own.

Being respectful of their privacy, I had done no more than peek into the brothers' rooms; even at my most melodramatic I could not imagine either one of them holding Doro captive in their own chambers. I also assiduously avoided the double doors at the end of the opposite hall, though—holding my breath as much as possible against that dreadful odor—I did inspect the rooms near it and found nothing but more dirt and neglect.

The ground floor was just as depressing. There was evidence of a once gracious life suddenly abandoned. I could almost feel the sad ghosts of a more congenial past as I explored the great, silent rooms. Everything to the smallest figurine was in place but covered with grime. Furniture as graceful and delicate as any I had known in the big houses of Savannah adorned two twin parlors. The material on one spindly chair had rotted, and I heard ominous squeaks coming from the rent. Mice, too! It was almost too much.

I am ashamed to admit that my courage would not take me into that kitchen again; however, I did venture into the butler's pantry and there found a treasure trove—shelves full of black objects that darkly reflected the gleam of my lamp. There must have been a king's ransom of silver silently tarnishing in that forgotten, dirty little room.

What manner of people were these Berkleys? They seemed to have no lack of money, yet they lived in squalor from which the poorest sharecropper would have recoiled. They traveled the world and apparently had many ships, but they could not keep a simple housemaid.

And my dear, missing Doro had loved one of them.

Chapter Nine

"MISS FARRADAY!"

I did wish Simon could have found me at a different time. Draped with cobwebs, one hand grasping the steep attic stair-rail and the other clutching the lamp, I was about as unimpressive a figure as could be imagined.

"Here, Mr. Berkley."

He looked at me and despite an heroic effort began to laugh. "My dear Miss Farraday, what have you been doing?"

"Exploring the attic," I replied with a damping dignity.

To be truthful, I had not really explored the attic. A curtain of cobwebs—whose creators I now feared were exploring my person—had obscured the way, and after I had reached the top of the stairs, my reward had been a silent floor whose carpet of velvety dust had never been disturbed. Doro could not be up there, for I didn't believe the Devil was abroad in Connecticut and not even the Berkleys could walk without tracks.

"Collecting spiders, it looks like," Simon replied with a laugh, removing one of the offending creatures from my shoulder and crushing it with his heel. "What on earth were you doing up there?"

"Your brother gave me his permission to look over the house in order to get an idea of what needs to be done."

Simon continued to pick sticky strands out of my hair. It was certainly an intimate attention which no gentleman should offer to a lady with whom he was but slightly acquainted, but at the moment I didn't particularly care. I have always had a particular dislike of spiders.

"And did you find your cousin?"

My brow furrowed in annoyance. Could these dratted Berkleys read my mind?

"Did you fear I might?"

By now we had reached the head of the stairs. I placed the lamp on the tall carved chest next to the bench and sank down. Leaning negligently on the chest as the lamplight picked out little sparkles of gold in his dark hair, Simon smiled down at me.

"Serious Miss Farraday! Do you never smile?"

"I have little to smile about, sir." A waft of the sweetish stench drifted past my nostrils, turning my stomach. I could not help but glance down that dimly lit corridor to the shadowy doors. From here I could not see the ferocious dragon carvings and I was just as glad. "I met Yu-Wei this afternoon. She seems most devoted to your mother."

"She's been with her since Mother came from China."

"It must be comforting for you to know that your mother is well cared for in her illness."

Simon shrugged. "I suppose. However, if she didn't have Yu-Wei pampering her all the time she might not choose to be ill."

Such callousness horrified me. What sort of creatures were these Berkleys, I wondered, and before I could stop myself, snapped "No one chooses to be ill! I find you and your brother's attitude quite incomprehensible."

"I don't know what dear brother Nicholas thinks, since he rarely has anything to do with her, but quite frankly she disgusts me."

"Mr. Berkley!" I cried in horror. "To speak so . . ."

"Ah, Miss Farraday! I see Simon has found you." Smiling urbanely, Nicholas stepped out of Simon's room; he walked slowly, but without his cane. He had changed into a dark suit, one so impressively cut that it would not have caused comment at the finest of Savannah parties. Starched linen, severe looking without the frosting of lace a Southerner would have worn, was relieved only by the winking of tiny red studs. They looked like rubies.

"I swear, brother, you overwhelm me with your elegance!" Simon teased, but I would have sworn there was an edge under his laughter.

"It is not polite to sit down in all your dirt when dining with a lady," he replied with a significant glance to Simon's riding clothes. In the pale lamplight, his scar hardly showed, and I would have been hard put to choose between the two brothers. "Even if the lady herself shows a partiality for it. What have you been doing, Miss Farraday?"

I should have known that any compliment would be barbed. "Exploring the house, sir. I should not think that you would object to dirt, as you have gone to the trouble of collecting such a great deal of it."

Nicholas threw back his head and laughed, then ruefully clapped a hand to his half-healed face. "We must be on our mettle every minute, Simon. I fear Miss Farraday is worth two of us. Tell the truth: where did you get so dirty?"

"In the attic, sir."

"Good God! What were you doing up there? I didn't think that place had been opened in years."

"I can assure you it has not, Mr. Berkley." Simon hadn't gotten all the spiders; at the moment one was making a slow progress down my back, but I would not give them the satisfaction of seeing me act like an hysterical female. I gritted my teeth.

"Obviously. Well, dinner is about to be served and you are in no fit state to eat it. Go change and see how much of that grime you can remove before you join us in the library."

It is a sign of the besetting sin of vanity that my first thought was of my looks. My good dress, my only other garment, was as much or more a mess than this one. Travel and dirt had all but rendered it unwearable; this one was festooned with cobwebs and calicoed with dirt. I was not fit company for Christians in either one.

"I appreciate your invitation, gentlemen, but I have nothing fit to wear. I shall have a tray in my room."

"Ridiculous," Simon said. "Simply brush away the worst of those cobwebs and come down."

"Really, sir, I cannot!"

"Nonsense." Nicholas's voice was stronger now. "If all you are worried about is a dress, you will find that Chang has freshened the one you wore yesterday. I believe it will be acceptable. Now go put it on and join us in the library."

Chang's work was most acceptable, indeed almost miraculous. The grey wool showed no sign of dirt, and only careful inspection showed a slight stain around the hem. The coarse lace of my bertha and cuffs had been carefully cleaned and I felt quite able—once I had washed my face, brushed my hair, and made a thorough inspection for additional spiders—to face polite society with equanimity. Even my poor linens had been washed. It had been a delicate attention on Nicholas's part.

I only wished I could rid myself of the nagging suspicion that it had been a good excuse to have my meagre luggage thoroughly searched.

Dinner that evening was quite a gay affair, considering. When I reached the library, Mrs. Webber was setting the small game table with heavy white ironstone from her own kitchen. A soup kettle, securely packed in hay, yielded up a homely fragrance of meat and vegetables. There was bread, as light and crusty as could be desired, and fresh yellow butter, and a hunk of whitish cheese. Simple fare, perhaps, but certainly an improvement over the past offerings of this house.

Nicholas sat behind the great desk, unconvincingly handling some papers. Simon was nowhere to be seen. A small, welcome fire crackled on the hearth, and strategically placed lamps managed to make the room almost cheerful despite the mournful soughing of the wind outside.

"Good evening, Miss Farraday," beamed Mrs. Webber, but though her mouth smiled there were clouds in her eyes. "How nice you look."

"Thank you. What a wonderful surprise! How did you manage it?" I inhaled deeply of the stew. One could almost draw sustenance from the odor.

"Oh, 'twas nothing to cook, miss, and then Webber brought everything up in a handcart. We'll be taking the dishes back as soon as you're done."

"You will do nothing of the sort. The weather out there is dreadful. I'm surprised it hasn't started to rain buckets already."

"It's just spattered a bit, miss. Not real weather."

"Real weather or not, you and Webber must go home now. I'll not have you caught in the rain." I wished that Nicholas would second my order, but he merely sat there, a sheaf of papers in his hand. The firelight cruelly highlighted his marred cheek, giving him a satanic look.

"But miss, what about the dishes? Who'll do them?"

"They can sit where they are or Chang can carry them to the kitchen. One more bit of disorder in this house won't make any difference tonight. Now you and Webber hurry home before the weather breaks."

"Well, if you aren't minding . . ."

"Of course not! Go along."

While I handed her her shawl, she told me of the bruise on the horse's rump. It was not cheering information. In my mind I had almost managed to put the incident down as sheer accident; now the dark clouds of doubt were growing again. It was possible that a stone kicked up from the road could have hit the horse and startled him, but it would be much more likely to have done so had we been traveling at a good pace. I didn't see how it could have hit the horse enough to startle it as slowly as we had been going.

My ruminations were cut short by the appearance of Simon. He, too, had changed into a suit as arresting as his brother's. Indeed, I felt quite cast into the shade by their magnificence and said so as we seated ourselves. Nicholas had been watching me narrowly during my last, whispered exchange with Mrs. Webber; Simon, approaching just as we had parted, had frowned outright. Despite their smiles and raillery, I felt uncomfortable.

"Then we must see about getting you some dinner clothes, Miss Farraday," Simon said easily, "though you look greatly improved at the moment."

"Anything would be an improvement over a veiling of cobwebs, Mr. Berkley," I returned with a smile. "However, I fear once things are more normal here I shan't have to worry about a dinner dress. I cannot help but feel that even here in the North it is *comme il faut* for the masters of the house to sit down to table with the housekeeper."

"Enough of that silliness," Nicholas said roughly. "You are no more a housekeeper than I."

"Why, sir, it was you who practically forced me into this career."

"Until we can restore you to your family."

My eyes, quite as determined as his, locked gazes with him. "Until I find my cousin, Mr. Berkley."

For a moment the air was tense. We were both strong-willed, and the clash that must someday come would surely be unpleasant. I don't think anyone had ever dared cross him!

Until now no one had touched their food. I could only assume that the men were paying me the compliment of allowing me to act as hostess, so I broke the tension by picking up my spoon and tasted my steaming bowl. The fragrance had not been misleading; it was ambrosial. I had not had anything so tasty since leaving Moonhaven.

"Ah, Mrs. Webber's stew!" breathed Nicholas, dipping into his soup. "I dreamed of this while lying out on that accursed heathen beach. You can't hold anything against a woman who cooks like this, Simon."

Simon patted his lips delicately with a napkin and took a sip of wine. "I never complained about her cooking. It was her stealing to which I objected. More wine, Miss Farraday?"

Whatever the shortcomings of Devon House, it possessed an admirable cellar. This was as good a Burgundy as I had ever tasted at Uncle Miller's, and he had been acknowledged as an authority.

"Just half a glass, please."

"Does it not please you?"

"Good heavens, no! It is excellent. It's only that tomorrow is going to be a very busy day, and I don't wish a fuzzy head."

"That is high praise indeed for our wine," said Nicholas with the hint of a smile. "Miss Farraday is something of a connoisseur. She recognized the Napoleon at once last night."

"She did?" Simon's voice was tinged with disbelief. "Imagine! A female who knows about spirits!"

I had my mouth open to reply when Nicholas forestalled me.

"Careful what you say, little brother. Our Miss Farraday is quite a speaker for the rights of women. She even wants the vote!"

Simon gazed at me as if I had suddenly grown another head. "Well, thank heavens that will never happen. God only knows in what shape that would put the country!"

"That is an illogical response, Mr. Berkley," I said spiritedly. "Women run homes all over the country, and I have even heard of a few who participate in commerce. Can you say that a well-educated woman is less capable than an ill-educated man?"

"I certainly can," Simon retorted. "A woman's brain may be very well for running a home, and perhaps there are a few freaks who have intruded into the business world, but you can't convince me a woman could understand the complexities of national concerns."

I was about to give a sharp rejoinder when Nicholas, who had been watching our exchange with amused eyes, placed a gentle hand on mine. "Perhaps we can test your theories of ability closer to home. What can you tell me about the horses bolting today?"

As the wretch had doubtless planned, that took me completely by surprise. I stammered momentarily, then took a strengthening sip of wine and tried to appear unruffled.

"I was not aware that you knew of that unfortunate incident, sir."

"Horses bolting? What's this all about?" Simon cried. "You never mentioned anything about this, Miss Farraday! Were you hurt?"

"No, none of us were." I looked from Simon's concerned face to Nicholas's rigid one. "How did you know of it, Mr. Berkley?"

He shrugged. "Surely you didn't expect Mrs. Webber to keep it a secret. Since the animals involved belong to the Berkleys, she thought we should know."

"So she told you, of course," Simon said bitterly before turning back to me with genuine concern in his eyes. "What happened, Miss Farraday? How did those idiots run away with you?" He gripped my hand. I am sure he meant only to be comforting, but it hurt. I extricated myself as gently as possible and told them the story. In retelling, I must admit it sounded sadly flat—as I had intended it to.

It did not take a great deal of intelligence to postulate that someone was unhappy with my persistence about Doro. By seeming to think nothing of the runaway incident, I hoped to lull the villain into a sense of false security. As Great-aunt Lorena had said so often, "Pride goes before a fall." If this unknown personage thought himself undetected, he would move more freely and therefore be more likely to make a mistake.

It did not contribute to my peace of mind to know that both of the Berkley brothers had been out riding that afternoon.

Chapter Ten

"YOU KNOW, MISS Farraday, you amaze me," Nicholas said easily, pouring himself another glass of wine.

The meal was over, and we sat sipping the last of the wine. Chang, his face as unreadable as ever, had quietly cleared the dishes, leaving only the wineglasses and the cheese, then produced a bowl of nuts which Simon took delight in cracking in his bare hands. Outside the rain had finally arrived in force and clawed incessantly at the windows.

I took the fractured nut Simon offered and began to pick out the chips of meat. "I, sir? Then you are easily amazed."

Another nut popped under Simon's fingers with a sound like breaking bone. "Admitted that our charming guest is an amazing creature, Nicholas, but what inspired that remark? Surely you cannot be just now noticing."

"Hardly, little brother. It is the lady's behavior which amazes."

I could not help it; I blushed. All in all, in running away from home, I had acted no better than a hoyden or even worse, no matter how unassailable my motives had been, but how unmannerly of this Yankee to mention it!

"I cannot see where my behavior is any of your concern, Mr. Berkley."

"It is when it concerns my servants."

"Confound it, Nicholas, stop being so mysterious. What are you trying to say?"

"You were not here to see Miss Farraday pack up Mrs. Webber and send her and Webber home so they wouldn't get wet."

"There was no need for them to stay," I answered defensively.

"Of course not, but your concern for mere servants is surprising.

Or do you regard them differently than the slaves on your southern plantations?"

Thinking of all the improvements Uncle Richard had made in the cabins in the last year, I bubbled with anger. The wretch was trying to pick a quarrel with me! Doubtless he was one of those tiresome abolitionists who raised a great deal of dust about something of which they knew nothing. Anger could never convince a person of his ilk how wrong they were, so I bit back the sharp words that bubbled on my lips and carefully picked out another nutmeat.

"You have been reading that dreadful *Uncle Tom's Cabin*," I said and was rewarded with a flash in his eyes. It was paradoxical; I was so glad that a book written by a woman could have such success among the literati, but during the six years it had been published, the totally inaccurate picture she had painted had caused us in the South a great deal of grief.

"You are familiar with it?"

Familiar! I could still see Aunt Belle's tears when she had first brought it home from the lending library and Uncle Miller's rage as he had quite deliberately torn it apart and burned the pieces. The entire town of Savannah had been in an uproar for weeks with the cooler heads advocating only tar and feathers. Only Great-aunt Lorena had seen it as both a tongue-in-cheek comedy of the finest proportions and, more seriously, perhaps the harbinger of the end of our way of life. She said most people had no sense of humor at all.

"Of course. We thought it monstrously funny. Don't tell me you took such a far-fetched tale seriously?" I asked with a dreadful archness.

His face darkened. "Didn't you?"

"Of course not. Mr. Berkley, most of our people have been born to the family. In a way, they are family."

"A cozy situation. Are they proud to be related to you?"

"Sarcasm does not become you, Mr. Berkley."

He nodded by way of apology and, over my protests, poured the last of the bottle into my glass. Already I had had more than I had intended to allow myself, but it was an excellent vintage, the like of which I had not tasted since leaving Uncle Miller's. I took an appreciative sip and, thus emboldened, spoke on, little realizing the sorrow my words would unwittingly cause.

"Besides, sir, even if you would discount such sentimentality, there is still the economic aspect."

Simon laughed nervously. "Economic aspect! Good Lord, Nicholas! What sort of thing do they teach girls down in the South? She sounds like old Wallingford."

"Our man of business at the shipyards," Nicholas supplied helpfully.

"A wonderful fellow," Simon added. "Quite bright about figures and such."

"But dry as dust."

I decided to ignore Mr. Nicholas Berkley's highly unflattering comparison. Obviously he was trying to bait me, and equally obvious I had not been invited to dinner as a guest, but rather as the entertainment.

"Figures do seem to be dry, if one does not understand them," I said with a sweet simper. Nicholas's eyes narrowed speculatively. "A good understanding of business would seem to be based in a good understanding of figures though."

I allowed my voice to drift off, then before either could speak, continued with a certain crispness. "However, gentlemen, we were speaking of slaves. All personal feelings aside, no owner in his right mind would voluntarily mistreat valuable property. Even the lowest field hand with no training at all is worth several hundred dollars. A skilled craftsman or house servant can be worth several thousand."

"I never thought blacks would bring so much." Simon's long fingers delicately picked a nutmeat and popped it into his mouth.

"Sometimes the price for a fancy piece is even more," I said boldly.

"And what do you know of fancy pieces?" Nicholas asked, but I sensed dangerous ground in that direction and forged on my own way.

"Forgive me for bringing this up, but you just lost a ship. I presume it was valuable?"

"Damned valuable." Nicholas said tersely.

"Did you deliberately wreck it?"

"Of course not!"

"Neither would a slave owner mistreat his valuable property, any more than you would deliberately damage one of your ships."

Simon drained his glass. "She's got you there, Nicholas. My compliments, Miss Farraday."

"But ships are not human beings. And despite your eloquence, I cannot agree with you. What about those who abuse their slaves, assets or no?"

"Yes, Miss Farraday," asked Simon. He was enjoying this greatly. Apparently he found the sight of his brother being bested amusing. For some reason I liked him a little less for that. "There must be some basis for the horrible tales we've heard. They can't all be made up."

I wanted to tell him yes, they were all fabrications of those who envied the graceful southern way of life, but I couldn't. Some of them, at least, I knew to be true.

"No," I answered, carefully throwing his own words back at him, "but there are doubtless a few who cannot understand the complexities of commerce."

Simon missed it completely, and had Nicholas not been unable to hide the slight twitch of his lips, I would have thought it had gone past him too. However, I was feeling charitable and made no sign that I saw.

"And of course, the slaves are not wood and steel, like your ships, which makes them that much more important. We take care of them, teach them trades and skills . . ."

"But not to read and write."

"What possible use could they have for that? Far better to learn cobbling and dressmaking."

"And fancy pieces?"

Something in his eyes made me uncomfortable and suddenly the game wasn't amusing any more. "That," I said with a crushing hauteur, "is something of which a lady does not speak."

No matter how outrageously a lady has behaved, any southern gentleman would have known that the subject was closed and

78

opened a new, less controversial one, but this infuriating Yankee would not be crushed! Instead, he laughed. Laughed! I would have sworn that he was now the one enjoying the unconventionality of the encounter.

And that made it that much harder to open the door to his mannerly knock later that night.

"Miss Farraday?"

"Who is it?"

"Nicholas Berkley."

My brush stopped mid-way through my hair, and I felt an unreasoning ripple of fear before common sense reasserted itself. First of all, if Nicholas Berkley had what Great-aunt Lorena would have called mischief on his mind, he probably wouldn't be knocking and if he really wanted to come in, a simple door and lock would not keep him out for long. And above all, I did not think him capable of such a scurrilous trick as forcing himself on a female under his protection. It was the least logical of all my reasons, yet it did more to convince me than anything else.

I opened the door only a crack, since I had already put on my nightgown and loosed my hair. He was still dressed, leaning heavily on his cane and carrying a single candle in a bedstick. It flared brightly against the darkness of the hall, casting the scarred side of his face into full shadow.

"Yes, Mr. Berkley?"

"I hate to disturb you, Miss Farraday, but I want to apologize for my behavior at dinner."

"There's no need."

"Indeed there is. I teased you unmercifully. My only excuse is that I have been too long away from the company of civilized people. I didn't mean to distress you."

It was a very pretty apology and one that he did not have to make. I thought it a most graceful gesture, yet still curiosity about the reasons which could have prompted it continued to bother me long after I had bade him good night, locked the door, and lain down for sleep.

* * *

The day dawned with a clamor like that of a crusade, with the forces of cleanliness and good fighting the forces of dirt and evil. Mrs. Webber and her three minions, their faces awestricken at the sight of Devon House, appeared wearing ancient dresses and headcloths such as the housegirls at home wore. Each carried a vicious-looking collection of mops and brooms and rags and buckets, ready to begin the good fight.

Luckily I was awake early and thus spared the embarrassment of being pulled heavy-eyed from bed, but my choice of clothes did not meet Mrs. Webber's approval. Since I could not very well clean in my petticoat, I had decided to sacrifice the tartan as a cleaning uniform, but one word from Mrs. Webber sent one of the girls scurrying back to her house for an old dress of her own that was, as she said, better suited to heavy work.

Indeed the dress had seen a great deal of heavy work, but it was clean and mended, and once an apron had been tied around me tightly enough to correct the difference between Mrs. Webber's girth and mine, it gave me a great deal of freedom of movement. A headrag was tied over my sensible braid, and at last I felt the equal of my comrades in battle; that is, I felt I looked quite as peculiar as they did.

Taking one look at our unlovely crew, Simon immediately wished us well and then said that he was riding out to visit some friends and would not be back until late. Following him more slowly down the stairs, Nicholas said that he would be busy with accounts in the library all day and that under no circumstances was he to be disturbed.

Here the fiction of my being housekeeper fell entirely apart. Her fingers twitching to get going in that disreputable kitchen, Mrs. Webber did not even pretend to wait for my orders; instead, she issued them herself with the confidence of a commanding general. I was banished from the kitchen area—"Too rough going for a lady," she said—and sent upstairs; the bedrooms were to be my charge, and I was to have Maud as a helper. "She's too frail for the heavy work we'll be needing," Mrs. Webber said grimly and, after counting out a measure of cleaning equipment for us to use, picked up her own implements, and charged forward.

I suppose it was just as well, for one of my highest priorities had been to obtain a room of my own. I had already decided on my chamber during my tour of the house. It was a small one near the stairwell and decently located as far from all members of the family as possible. Not only was it comfortable, but should I decide to do some after-hours exploring, my departure would not disturb the family. The housekeeper's room should, I suppose, have been downstairs somewhere near the kitchen, but nothing would induce me to sleep in that realm of the rat and the black beetle!

We waded in with a will, and, as the room was nearly presentable by lunch, I felt I had confirmed a suspicion that had been growing since my first tour of the house. Downstairs in the reception rooms, the dirt was crusted thickly, mute evidence of long neglect, but the bedchambers, while far from clean, responded to an easy touch. Here the dirt was more on the surface, which led me to think that either these rooms had been occupied until a short time ago, or the former staff of Devon House had had some very peculiar attitudes regarding cleaning.

Lunch had been a cold pick-up affair that first day, and, though I was ready to drop with weariness, I changed and sat down to dinner with the Berkley brothers. They had requested my presence in tones that left no doubt as to it being an order. Between the heat of the library fire and the excellent wine which Nicholas had selected, it was all I could do to keep my eyes open and my face out of my plate.

"I don't know how you stood it here today, Nicholas," Simon said and gulped his wine. "I for one feel like abandoning ship until this upheaval is over."

"Surely a captain does not desert his ship."

Simon grinned lazily. "Ah, but you are captain here now, not I. I am merely biding time until I leave for China."

"Have you had news of the *Evening Star?*"

"Yes, she was posted at the chandler's shop today. She docked at the shipyards two days ago."

"Any damage?"

"Nothing serious. Lost some rigging in a gale, and she needs caulking, but she'll be ready to go in ten days or so and then I'm off to the Far East!" Simon's eyes glittered.

"It must be a wondrous thing to see the world," I murmured, trying to keep a sense of the conversation. "Have you been there before?"

"Yes. I spent one year as company manager and before that took several trips as a boy."

"Meaning that you ran away from school and stowed away on one of our ships. Poor old Carstairs had a devil of a time with you. Carstairs was our guardian," Nicholas added.

"Simply because I was not a grind who looked no further than the edges of his schoolbooks."

Even half-asleep, I could feel the tension building in the air. Old quarrels were the worst. "What a worry you must have been to your mother."

"Our mother could have cared less."

Simon's harshness shocked me. "I hadn't know her illness was of such long standing."

"Her illness began the day our father died."

My confusion must have shown, for although Nicholas grimly contemplated his wineglass, he spoke to me. "I gather that you do not know the true nature of our mother's illness. Mother is an opium-eater."

Opium! That accounted for the peculiar sweet stench which emanated from Mrs. Berkley's rooms and for her singular lack of courtesy in not greeting me either as guest or housekeeper. It was possible she didn't even know I was here.

"When our father died she wanted no more to do with the world or with us. She could not stand to live without him."

Suddenly I understood their point of view and was embarrassed for my harsh thoughts towards them. While it has been a hard thing to come through life never knowing the security or warmth of a mother's love, how much worse it must be to carry in your heart the knowledge that your mother lived and yet rejected you. I felt ashamed.

"I'm sorry. I didn't know," I said, but neither of them answered. There was nothing to say.

Chapter Eleven

BY THE SECOND day I could see a great deal of progress. Mrs. Webber and her girls had the kitchen in almost perfect condition, so much so that Charity was left to finish up while Mrs. Webber and Alice turned their attention to the downstairs rooms. Maud was scrubbing in one bedroom while I put the final touches on the one just finished. We were going a great deal faster than I had anticipated, despite the lack of cooperation from Yu-Wei and Chang.

All the girls were terrified of the Chinese, and small wonder. Both had a nasty habit of moving soundlessly, so that when you thought you were alone and turned around, there one of them was, quietly standing not two feet from you.

It was unnerving, to say the least.

While Maud and I had been busy in the corridor, moving our equipment and the like, Yu-Wei had stood at the door of her mistress's room like a guard dog. Whenever Maud and I even looked like we were going to come that way, she had shaken her fist and muttered something in her native tongue, daring us to come any nearer. Poor Maud got so she would not set foot in the passage unless I was with her.

I didn't mind, thinking her fears overblown, until the time I had passed Simon's door and been startled half out of my wits by the sudden appearance of Chang. The tiny slits of his eyes were barely visible beneath his frown, but they emitted a malevolent gleam.

"You go 'way," he snarled. "No come here. Never come here."

After that I was less intrepid about walking alone, yet Simon, when I taxed him with it before he departed for his morning ride, merely laughed.

"It's nothing, Miss Farraday. They've been the only ones here for so long they resent change. They'll come around," he said dismissively. Then, seeing that my worry did not disperse, his face softened and he laid a gentle hand on my arm. "I'll speak to them."

I went back to work feeling somewhat more secure, and whatever Simon said to them must have worked, for after that I caught only rare glimpses of either Chinese, though I never did lose the feeling of dark, alien eyes watching my every move.

The first surprise of the morning came in a small bedroom near the back of the house. I privately called it the nurse's room, for it was just next to the nursery.

Whoever the nurse had been, she had not had much in the way of comfort. A narrow bed, a straight-backed chair, a washstand that leaned precariously, and a giant armoire half the size of the room were the only furnishings. Perhaps the room had been changed since the young Berkleys had needed a nurse, or perhaps she had been too busy taking care of two lively little boys to notice the lack of her own comfort; I hoped it was the former, for as it was this room was grim.

Then I opened the towering armoire.

The interior was not festooned with spiderwebs as the others had been; in fact, this unattractive old piece appeared to have been recently used, as the crumpled heap of fabric in the bottom attested. As I reached for it, my skin began to prickle in warning.

It was a very pretty dress, and it had not been lying at the bottom of this ancient armoire for too long. The style was quite new, and although wrinkled the material was fresh. I held it against me; it had been made for a smaller girl. The waist would never enclose mine, and the hem missed the floor by a full three inches, but the color . . . The color! My heart was beating erratically. The color was a rich, pure green, the shade most flattering to redheads.

Even though it was cold in the many-windowed nursery, I didn't feel the chill. I had gone in there to think, unable to stay in the small, ugly room where I had found my cousin Doro's green dress. Yes, I was as certain that that dress had belonged to Doro as I was of anything I had ever known in my life. Some inner knowledge, some surety of blood and bone told me that Doro had worn that dress and at some time she had hidden it there. In hope of what?

There was no proof, nothing that would convince anyone but me. I had gone over that dress seam by seam, searching for any form of identification that would positively link it to Doro, but there had been nothing; merely a new, well-made dress stuffed in the bottom of an old armoire in an abandoned room.

"Sad, isn't it?"

I jumped.

"I'm sorry, Miss Farraday. I didn't mean to startle you." Nicholas's dark eyes were full of concern. "Are you all right?"

Dare I tell him? I thought not; there was nothing really to connect Doro with that dress. Convincing him would take more definite evidence.

"I'm fine. You did startle me, though. What did you say?"

He looked over the dusty nursery: the school tables piled one on another, the rocking horse with no tail, the tall screen folded in the corner.

"I said this was sad. Simon and I were raised here, you know. We were the only two children to use it."

I recalled the crowded nurseries of my childhood. "That is a shame. It's so spacious."

I was sitting in the windowseat, and he took a place beside me. Beyond the windows was the apron of the back lawn and then nothing but the sea. It was an hypnotic view, even on such a lackluster day. In the spring, when the sky was bright blue and the wind was fresh, it would be beautiful. I could imagine Nicholas and Simon as children playing in this room.

"Yes, old Cecil built for a dynasty," he snorted bitterly. "Some dynasty. Come and gone in two generations."

"Cecil?"

"My grandfather. You know our family history?"

Who could forget it? Kidnapping, the curse of an old island woman, a suicide . . . I looked away. "My driver told me."

"I'm not surprised. No one comes to this part of the country without hearing at least one version of it. Old Cecil planned to build an empire."

"And it seems he succeeded," I said innocently. "There is this house and your company . . ."

"You cheer me, Miss Farraday," he said, but his laugh didn't sound at all happy. "The eternal, courageous optimist. Damaged trees bring forth rotten fruit," he added cryptically.

His expression was so haunted and hurt I wanted only to comfort him, which was in itself ridiculous, for I never met a man in my life who needed comforting less than Nicholas Berkley. Still, the bleakness in his eyes was painful.

I gripped his cold hand with my own. "Please, Mr. Berkley, it can't be that bad." I didn't know what else to say, but it appeared to have been the right thing. He patted my hand, and the clouds in his face cleared somewhat.

"You are most kind, Miss Farraday," he said and in that instant I felt as if a wave of dizziness washed over me, yet I wasn't dizzy. There was a peculiar feeling in the pit of my stomach and for a moment I couldn't catch my breath. It was a most unpleasant sensation, and, though I had never experienced it before, it felt oddly familiar.

The opening door caught us entirely unaware. We jumped apart as if we had been doing something we shouldn't, and nothing makes one look more guilty than acting so!

"Oh, mum, I'm sorry." Maud goggled at us.

"It's quite all right," I answered in Aunt Evelyn's best voice. "What did you want?"

She extended a very dirty square of once white cambric. "It's this, mum. You must have dropped it. I was scrubbing in the next room and found it. Right jammed up under the dresser, it was."

"Thank you," I murmured, but she was already gone.

Again that peculiar prickle danced across my skin as I unfolded the wrinkled handkerchief. My hands shook. There was an elaborate *D* embroidered in the corner; that was why Maud had thought it mine, but I had never owned anything so fine as this. This was not my handkerchief.

It had to be Doro's.

"You have done well with the house."

"I beg your pardon?"

"You have done well with this house. It seems I underestimated you and for that I apologize. I never thought to see it taking shape so quickly. Tell me, what have you done with the little Chinese pieces?"

The enormity of the evidence in my hand seemed to have stifled my wits. I could not concentrate on what he was saying. "Chinese pieces, sir?"

"Yes. I looked in the upstairs rooms while trying to find you, and I wondered what had happened to the decorations. There were a number of things my father brought back, like the things in my room."

"The rooms were much as you saw them, sir. I don't remember any Chinese decorative objects." My fingers closed convulsively over the handkerchief. Should I tell him? Would he believe me? This was absolute proof to me that Doro had been in this house, but might he think it was mine? "There seem to be a great number of things in the parlors, perhaps they were taken down there."

He looked sad. "No, those things aren't Chinese; my grandmother brought them from the islands when she was a bride. Oh, well, it makes no matter. The reason I was looking for you was to ask if any of the bedrooms are suitable for use."

"Yes, sir, if the inhabitant is not too finicky. I can have the corner room ready in an hour or so. At least its chimney is clear and appears to be in working order."

"The corner room will be fine and I assure you old Wallingford is not the least finical in his ways."

"The man with the figures?"

"All dry as dust, too." He smiled briefly. "There are some legal matters which we must settle before Simon leaves for China. Can the household stand a guest for a day or two?"

"Certainly it can. Mrs. Webber has the kitchen well in hand, if he does not object to plain cooking, and I can guarantee him a habitable room." The handkerchief burned my hand. Carried away on a wave of trust, I decided to trust him. My fingers clenched, crushing the initialed fabric. "Doro—"

It was as far as I got, for no sooner had I started to speak than a dreadful shrieking arose from the regions below, sounding indeed like one of the damned being carried away into the maw of Hell itself.

Chapter Twelve

DESPITE HIS INJURED leg, Nicholas was far ahead of me as we dashed into the kitchen. Now it was a completely different room from the filthy horror I had originally seen; scrubbed within an inch of its life, it fairly glowed with soap and wax. There were only two small windows, but now they sparkled when the weak sun hit them. The stone counters were spotless and though the cabinet doors were shut I knew that behind them perfect order reigned. There, however, order seemed to end. We stood on the edge of a war.

Mrs. Webber stood in the center of the kitchen, her face alight with martial fire as she wielded a chair like a shield. Behind her, still screaming like a scalded cat, Alice knelt in a pathetic huddle, her fingers convulsively caught in Mrs. Webber's skirt. Across the kitchen, frozen into an attitude of an animal at bay, crouched a snarling Chang, a small, wicked-looking knife raised high.

"What is going on here?" I cried just as Nicholas spat something in the Chinese tongue. Chang stepped back from Nicholas and tightened his grip on the knife. For a moment my breath stopped. It looked like they were going to come to blows over the weapon.

Straight as a ship's mast, Nicholas stepped between Chang and us, offering his body as a shield for our protection. It was thrilling to see him advance fearlessly on the cowering manservant, his empty hand firmly outstretched. I had never seen such a demonstration of raw courage; I feared for Nicholas—for what match was an unarmed convalescent against a knife's edge?—yet I also thrilled at such selfless heroism.

For a moment, time seemed to stop until Nicholas broke the spell by repeating his order, and this time it worked. Chang seemed to shrink as he gently laid the dagger in his master's outstretched palm.

"What happened, Mrs. Webber?" I asked, surprised to find that my voice squeaked.

"That heathen was soft-footing around behind my back, Miss Farraday!" Her shelf-like bosom trembled with indignation. Under her outraged tones, I could hear the soft fluting of Chang's voice as he spoke ingratiatingly to Nicholas.

Mrs. Webber and I got the whimpering Alice off the floor and into the chair. I could hardly blame the girl for being afraid, but she was so debilitated by her fright she could do little but sit and shiver. Somehow such lack of gumption irritated me, as it always had in my cousin Eula. I had found it disgusting, but Eula had always said that I had none of the finer sensibilities. If that were the result, I didn't want them. Luckily, Alice had a core of sterner stuff, and, after a few bracing words, she picked herself up and sidled out of the kitchen.

Mrs. Webber drew a deep breath. "There's something I must tell you, Miss Farraday. Today's the first time I can say for sure, but there's food missing again."

"Again? Are you positive?" My heart sank. When this came to Simon's ears, he would demand Mrs. Webber's removal and I would be lost without her.

"To be sure I would know if there was half a meat pie missing! I was planning to serve the last of it tonight, along with some toasted cheese, and some sort of vegetable. Seeing as it was getting sort of chilly, I thought you'd be wanting a substantial meal. And it's gone! And that's not all, Miss Farraday. We brought back two big sacks of rice, and one of them's fair empty already."

"But that must have held twenty-five pounds or more!"

"Aye, it did, but it's gone now." She shot a darkling look at Chang, who was now cringing under the edge of Nicholas's tongue. Considering their expressions, I was extremely glad I didn't speak the language.

"But why was he threatening you with a knife?"

"I was at the table, scraping the potatoes to make a nice nourishing soup for tomorrow, when I asked Alice to get some onions. I should have looked myself when she said she didn't see any in the larder—though they really were in there all the time and were just behind the potatoes—and that she was going to look in the cellar."

The cellar. I had made a cursory inspection of it; cold, dank, and cut into the very rock of the earth itself, it was a surprisingly small room reached only by a rickety staircase from the kitchen. The walls and floor were shiny with wet, and a number of large bugs had run frantically from the oncoming light. A few rotted shelves had lined the walls, and an enormous pile of coal had filled fully half the space. Aside from that, the only thing of note was a heavily bolted door that no amount of tugging could open. Mrs. Webber had said it had once led to a path to the shoreline, but that years before the Captain had ordered the passage sealed. Stonemasons and plasterers had worked for days in the cellar, and the old door had been left simply because it was too heavy to remove. It certainly looked as if it hadn't been disturbed in years. The wines were kept in a separate cellar, a tiny room accessible only from the library.

"The cellar? Anything would rot quickly down there."

"I know that, but you know the girl isn't smart. Anyway, she went down there, then started screaming like she was being skinned alive. She came charging up those stairs and that heathen was right behind her, waving that knife."

"I wonder what Chang was doing down there?" I mused, accepting Mrs. Webber's story as gospel. Several days of working with her had convinced me she was as truthful a person as I could ever hope to know, which made Simon's allegations that much more confusing.

"Humph! Some devil's work, no doubt. I didn't even hear that soft-footed heathen go down there!"

"Did you ever see a Chinese dagger, Miss Farraday?" Nicholas had come up behind me without our notice; apparently he too had learned the Chinese ability of walking without being heard.

I gasped as he shoved the cold metal handle into my hand. It was a beautiful thing; the blade was dull steel, wickedly sharp and businesslike, but the handle was an object of art. Formed in the shape of a tree stump, it was intertwined with climbing vines; the vines themselves had delicate flowers and the center of each flower was a tiny, winking gem.

"It's beautiful!" I cried, trying to see it only as a delicate piece of art instead of a possible instrument of death. "Is it part of your family collection?"

He shook his head. "I don't recall ever seeing it before. Some high-born Chinese ladies used to carry them . . . sort of a sign of rank. Now, what was all this about?"

In as brief a version as possible, I told him what Mrs. Webber had told me, leaving out the stolen food. I intended to investigate that myself, and hopefully it would not come to Simon's ears until I had some proof one way or the other. Of course Mrs. Webber noticed the omission, but kept silent, nodding in agreement as I sketched the facts.

"And what reason does that heathen give for scaring poor Alice nearly to death?" she asked when I was finished.

"He says that he was down there getting supplies for his mother's altar when Alice came down and tried to kill him."

"Alice?" we women chorused. "That's impossible," I said while Mrs. Webber growled, "She hasn't got the intelligence to kill a fly!"

"And," I added, "what on earth could he be storing down in that damp, ugly cellar? And what altar?"

"His mother keeps some sort of shrine in her room. It's part of their religion."

"Heathen!" snorted Mrs. Webber, but Nicholas continued as if he hadn't heard.

"Apparently he keeps the joss sticks down there. Maybe the damp helps keep them from drying out."

It made a sort of sense. I had seen the joss sticks, long threadlike affairs coated with a sweetish incense which those affected by Oriental ways are prone to burn at any time. Some believed the fumes drove away devils. They burned nearly constantly in Mrs. Berkley's suite, perhaps as an attempt to cover up the sweeter, more sickly odor of the opium. Of course, the simple expedient of opening a window never appeared to occur to anyone, so the commingled scents made an overpowering perfume. Even the brothers used joss sticks, for their not unpleasant odor often filled the library, and in most rooms of the house there was at least one of the curiously designed holders. Nearly every one, I might add, was in the shape of a dragon.

"Do you think she just startled him, and he's making up that story to cover his overreaction?"

"Humph!" Mrs. Webber exploded. "He just wanted to make mischief again!"

Nicholas nodded slowly at her outburst. "I think you might be right, Mrs. Webber. If only he would go to China with Simon," Nicholas mused, "but he'd never go without his mother."

"Send them both," Mrs. Webber said stoutly. "We can find a good Christian to look after Mrs. Berkley."

"Yu-Wei has been with Mother since she married," Nicholas said. "I don't know if she'd accept someone else."

"I won't have that heathen frightening my girls, Master Nicholas. I agreed to come back for you and your mother's sake, but I won't put up with a sneaking Chinee trying to stab my help!"

"And you won't have to," Nicholas said, trying to pacify. "I don't know just what I'll do, but you won't be bothered again. Ladies." With an abbreviated nod of the head he was gone, his brow furrowed with thought.

In the melee, I had forgotten to mention Doro's handkerchief, and it would be a long time before there would be another opportunity.

Mr. Wallingford arrived later that afternoon. A spare, wizened little man, he accepted the Spartan accommodations and the transitional status of Devon House without comment and seemed more interested in his books and ledgers—of which he had brought an amazing amount—than in the simple, wholesome meals Mrs. Webber set forth. One could hardly imagine a more undemanding guest.

Doro's handkerchief joined her bertha and dress beneath my mattress. I knew it was a simple hiding place, but the best I could devise. No opportunity to show any of them to Nicholas had

93

presented itself, so I merely kept my silence as I had all along, and the possibility of our collaboration passed.

Mr. Wallingford was with us for three days and a strange time it was, too. He and Nicholas spent hours closeted in the library, sometimes not stopping even for the meals that we carried in on trays. Sometimes Simon joined them, more often not; when he was not closeted with them he rode out into the country, coming in occasionally to eat. He wore a dark expression most of the time and once did not see me at all until our paths had quite literally collided.

"Oh, Miss Farraday!" he cried, at once bending to pick up the scattered linens that had occupied my attention until the last moment. "I am so sorry. Are you all right?"

He said it with such sincerity that I instantly forgot my trodden-upon toes in the glow of his smile. He had just come in; he was dressed for riding, and his clothes were liberally spattered with fresh mud.

"I'm fine, Mr. Berkley. And you," I asked suddenly, "are you all right?"

"Surely you don't fear you have injured me, Miss Farraday?" His voice was soft, and the look in his eyes gave me a strange, rather fluttery feeling in the region of my stomach. "I have taken many harder hits than that."

Driven by the haunted look in his eyes, I gathered my courage and plunged on. If we had not met in the intimacy of the shadowy upper hall, if he had not looked so dashingly handsome and yet so vulnerable, I probably would have kept my peace. However, keeping my mouth shut has always been a difficult task!

"Mr. Berkley—you look troubled."

Gently he cupped my chin with his hand. "Dear, kindhearted Miss Farraday! Would you relieve me of my problems?"

"I would help if I could, sir."

"I believe you would," he said in quite an odd tone, then a frown crossed his brow. "I thank you for your concern, but there's nothing to be done now. First he bleeds the company dry, then makes a big show of trying to save it. . . ." His voice faded away.

"I don't understand. Mr. Wallingford?"

"No," he answered harshly. "My dear brother Nicholas. Siphons off every available penny to China, then demands an accounting. And old Wallingford backs him every step of the way. I can't get a word in. It's hard to see the family business bled to the point of death, Miss Farraday. I'm just glad my father isn't alive to see it."

"Mr. Berkley sent everything to China?"

"Of course. He just came from there, didn't he? And I'll bet that none of the money taken from company accounts here has ever shown up in a company account there!"

"Surely there must be records."

"Records can easily be changed. He's saying that I did it, and the records back him up." He made an ugly sound of disgust.

"You? Why?"

"Because only one of us can draw funds of that amount from the company, and he doesn't want his name on it."

"But if he had the money over there, why did he come back?"

"What better way to avoid suspicion? Besides, while I am gone there is a great deal that can be finished up here." Simon shrugged and looked mournfully around him as if trying to impress the scene on his memory. "I wonder if there will be anything left by the time I return?"

"Surely there is something that can be done."

"Dear Miss Farraday," he said, and his eyes softened. "If I were only going to China under happier conditions—if I thought—" His hand stroked my cheek gently, then surprisingly he bent to place gentle lips on my forehead.

Heaven only knew where we would have gone from there, for my heart had begun to pound in a most agitated fashion, but at that moment, Nicholas appeared at the head of the stairs. Compared to Simon's glow of health, he looked old, and, as he stalked down the hall toward us, his limp was more pronounced than ever. For some reason I thought of Apollo and Vulcan; it was surely an exaggerated comparison, but Nicholas's expression was quite as black as the blacksmith god's had ever been.

"Simon! Damn it all, man, we've been waiting the better part of the morning for you."

"It seems like you and Wallingford have already decided on the answers, Nicholas. You don't need me."

"You are as much a member of this company and this household as I am, and damn you, you'll take your part in running it!"

Simon's eyes flashed, and I wished myself a thousand miles away. It was bad enough to be caught in the middle of this family quarrel without having been found being kissed like one of the housegirls! There weren't even enough shadows to cover my blushes.

"What there is left of it."

"You're a fine one to talk like that! When I left, the shipyard was a growing concern, and the house was habitable. I come back and find near-bankruptcy and a ruin!"

"Gentlemen, gentlemen . . ." Attracted by the loud voices, Mr. Wallingford peeped out from the stairwell. "Surely we can handle this in a civilized manner."

It was too late for such advice. The quarrel between the brothers had been building up since before either Mr. Wallingford or I appeared on the scene—perhaps even from childhood, for all I knew—and soft words from an outsider would have little effect. Not since Nicholas's encounter with Chang days before had I seen such a tense attitude of confrontation between two men, and I was irrationally glad that this time there was no golden Chinese dagger present to tempt them, for Simon was no Chang to bend before his brother's will.

"What have you done, Simon? Where is the money from the shipyard? Damn your eyes, where is the Chinese collection that our father made?"

Two pairs of dark eyes, eerily alike, glittered with angry light. Mr. Wallingford and I glanced at each other uneasily. If they came to blows, what could we do? A slightly built older man and a young woman would be no match for two young giants bent on destruction. And Nicholas was crippled. . . .

"Damn your eyes, Nicholas, you should be answering that question. And about the collection, why don't you ask your precious Mrs. Webber? I took over the house the way you left it. . . ."

Something had to be done. Perhaps they could live through such a nerve-wracking confrontation, but I certainly couldn't!

"Stop it!" I shouted melodramatically and stepped in between them. As far as it went, it was a magnificent gesture, something on the lines of a lamb challenging elephants, and miracle of miracles, it worked. Both looked at me with startled surprise, as if they had forgotten I was there, but the unbearable tension was broken.

"You're right, Miss Farraday. Nicholas, this is an unseemly way to be handling our business." Simon nodded to Mr. Wallingford. "Shall we go to the library?"

They departed, but Nicholas hung back until they had disappeared down the stairwell. Gathering up the stack of linens that had unwittingly been the cause of the confrontation, I watched him come back with a trembling eye. Was I to be chastised? Fired? Thrown out?

"Thank you, Miss Farraday," he said in rough tones. "That took courage."

"It was nothing, sir," I lied stoutly, hoping that my voice did not tremble as much as my knees.

"In the future, stay out of things that don't concern you. And stay away from Simon," he added angrily before he spun on his heel and stamped away.

Chapter Thirteen

I NEVER REALLY knew what happened in that last conference between Mr. Wallingford and the Berkley brothers, but when Mr. Wallingford left the next morning, there was at least an atmosphere of civility between the two. Even after Mr. Wallingford's departure, they remained closeted in the library. Mrs. Webber took in their meals, and I was thankful that no autocratic summons came for me to join them at dinner. I could not have faced either of them with composure.

Besides that, I was tired. During their days of work in the library, I had not been idle. Finding Doro's handkerchief and dress had galvanized me to action. I searched as much of the house as I could once more, this time tapping walls for any hidden doors and examining fireplaces and any other place I could think of for secret entrances—all, I might add, with a singular lack of success.

Even the food thief evaded me. In an attempt to dissuade the culprit, I made obvious level marks on all the containers and a listing of every dish; it did no good. Then, after convincing myself of the cellar's impenetrability, I carried everything down there, locked the door, and carried the key on my person, never allowing anyone down there without my presence.

The very evening of the Berkley brothers' confrontation, Mrs. Webber requested a measure of coffee for the morrow's breakfast. I had unlocked the door, and we crept down the stairs to find that a goodly chunk of roast and at least a pound of rice had vanished.

"I never!" Mrs. Webber declared. She looked in bags and under covers, but the viands were unmistakably gone. Wearily, I gave the order that all foodstuffs should be moved back into the more convenient larder in the morning. A thief that could creep through locked doors or pass through stone walls could not be stopped. Depressed at all my failures, I declined dinner and sought the solitude of my room.

I stripped off the enveloping housedress and readied myself for bed. Again I wished that I had brought Doro's letters, for it was becoming of paramount importance which Berkley brother she had loved—sedate, scarred Nicholas or gentle, laughing Simon. Both had qualities that were eminently loveable, yet one or both of them were lying. And I feared I was no longer as impartial as I should have been. It shamed me to admit it, but, when I should have been thinking of nothing but the necessity of finding Doro, my mind willfully drifted off to a pair of dark eyes and a ravaged face.

Yes, my mind dwelt on Nicholas. I cannot say why of the two brothers he engaged my fancy, but I found his image invading my thoughts at the most inappropriate times. There was something, some indefinable something about the essence of the man that called to an undiscovered part of me. My time away from Moonhaven was not very long, but in that short time I had changed quite a bit.

I finished tying my hair in its loose sleeping braid and blew out the candle. Doro or no Doro, there was no use wasting time mooning over Nicholas. Part of my depressed mood had to be attributed to his attitude; he regarded me solely as a tiresome dependent, almost as a property to be watched over until I could be returned to my rightful owner. His only feeling for me as an individual was an amused kind of tolerance and to try to read anything else into his civility was foolish. I eased myself between the covers and lay back, glad to be able to rest my weary body and to know that at least in sleep I need not feel I should discipline my thoughts against Nicholas Berkley.

Not being used to such hard labor, I found dropping off easy and was sound asleep when the dreadful shrieking began.

At first, in the disorientation of startled half-sleep, I thought it was Mammy Esther conjuring the voodoo again until I remembered that Mammy Esther had been gathered to her forefathers years ago and could never call on the fearful Baron Samedi and his undead again, at least, not from this world. I could not imagine why those horrible memories had returned to haunt me now.

Then, as I finally surfaced into full wakefulness, I realized that the air was still full of that dreadful wailing. Dear heaven, that tortured sound was coming from a human throat! And—what might be worse—it was in the house itself.

No shred of moonlight penetrated my chamber, and the box of wax vestas on the bedside table skittered away from my anxious fingers. I heard them hit the floor, but there was no time to search for them while there was so much misery abroad. Throwing my shawl over my nightgown, I ran to the door, managing to hit an amazing amount of furniture in the process.

Blessedly, there was a light in the hallway.

Nicholas, minus his jacket but otherwise dressed as he had been at dinner, stood at the head of the stairs, a branched candelabra held high. Simon emerged from his room carrying a single candle, the tie of his robe half-knotted. Both the bright color and fabric of his dressing gown proclaimed its eastern origins, and I wasn't even surprised to see that it was thickly embroidered with dragons.

The far end of the hallway resembled one of the old engravings of Hell. The great double doors stood open, allowing a spill of light to illuminate the area. The air was thick with the nauseating stench, and thin tentacles of smoke drifted like fog, combining with the grey light to give the carved dragons a dreadful semblance of life. Two figures struggled in the middle of this fantastic scene. Both were as small as children, but their faces showed their age, so the whole effect was of two trolls locked in mortal combat. The figure in the boxy jacket and trousers could only be that of Yu-Wei; the frail figure with the rat's-nest of flying hair had to be Mrs. Berkley. She was still screaming.

"Stop it!" I cried, flying forward to separate the two. For all their seeming fragility, there was a lot of strength in those four small hands. I had to pry Yu-Wei's scrawny claws from Mrs. Berkley, then gasped as simultaneously the poor old lady clung to me like a desperate child, and the Chinese woman struck at me with her fists.

"You go away!" she shrieked, her blows surprisingly vicious. "Leave Missee to me! She mine! She mine!"

Unable to counter the woman's blows, I twisted about, trying to shield the pathetic Mrs. Berkley as best I could. She was still shrieking, begging me to protect her, to take her away.

It couldn't have lasted as long as I thought it did, nothing could have. Nicholas and Simon pulled the Chinese woman away, but when they released her she flew at me again, still yelling, as if she would pull the old woman away by force, which in turn sent Mrs. Berkley's screams even higher. The sickeningly sweet stench became an entity in itself, swirling thickly about us until I felt like screaming myself.

Finally, with Simon holding her tightly and Nicholas repeating his firm order to be silent both in English and in Chinese, the servant woman was subdued. In another moment I had Mrs. Berkley's screams quieted to a continual low whimper by the same expedient of holding her scrawny body tightly and stroking her hair like a child.

"Now," Nicholas said, not even trying to hide the disgust in his voice, "what is the meaning of this, Yu-Wei?"

The blaze of hatred was completely gone from the old woman's eyes now, leaving her face nothing more than an impassive golden mask. "I sorry, sir. Missee have bad time."

"If you are no longer able to control my mother's outbursts . . ."

Her face hidden deep in my neck, Mrs. Berkley began a soft moaning that tore at my soul.

"Sorry, sir, just one time bad time."

By this time Simon had released her and moved away slightly. His face wore the same expression of disgust as his brother's, and I hated them both for it.

"Really, Yu-Wei, all we ask you to do is to keep her calm." Simon's voice was cold. "We can't have these upsets."

"Not happen again, sir. I take care Missee. No more noise. . . ."

"There'd better not be," Nicholas said grimly.

Not once had either of them looked at their mother. I couldn't stand it. Whatever her failings, Mrs. Berkley was their mother, and only one who had grown up without one could fully understand what that meant.

"Really, Mr. Berkley!" I said with impartial anger. "Your mother is ill. . . ."

Nicholas turned to face me, and, though his face was rigid with disapproval, there was agony in his eyes. "My mother has been ill for many years, Miss Farraday. Give her back to Yu-Wei and hope we can get some sleep tonight."

The golden mask unchanging save for a glitter deep in her eyes, Yu-Wei reached for Mrs. Berkley, and the instant those claw-like hands came toward her, Mrs. Berkley began that dreadful wailing again, only this time it came out studded with slurred words.

"No! No! Not hurt! Go away!" and she clung to me with arms of steel.

"Come, Missee," Yu-Wei said firmly. "You mine."

There was some quality in her voice, or perhaps in her eyes, that sent shivers through me. I should not like to be under that creature's care. Perhaps some of Mrs. Berkley's fear had communicated itself to me, but I knew then I would never again voluntarily release the poor wreck to the Chinese woman.

"No!" I shouted and my outburst surprised everyone else almost as much as it did me. "I'll take care of Mrs. Berkley."

"Missee mine," Yu-Wei repeated grimly. "My responsibility."

"That isn't necessary, Miss Farraday," Simon said with a surprising gentleness. "Mother has these spells from time to time. Yu-Wei knows how to handle them."

I tightened my grip on the old lady. She was quivering under my hands like a captured bird. "But there must be some reason . . ."

Nicholas's face was a mask of disgust, redeemed only by the pain in his eyes. "It was about this time of year that our father died. Mother has always become unmanageable when the date comes."

"Come! Missee mine." Again the yellow claws reached out, and Mrs. Berkley began to keen once more, a high, shrill sound that chilled the blood. Yu-Wei reached out and clamped a hand on the thin, aged shoulder. Acting with instinctive revulsion, I brushed it away as I would a loathsome reptile.

"Please," I cried desperately, appealing to both the brothers, "let me take her. Can't you see she's frightened?"

"Miss Farraday, my mother is an opium addict." Nicholas spoke slowly, as if each word cut his mouth.

"What Nicholas is trying to say is that she's unpredictable," Simon added. There was pain in his eyes too.

"I take care. Missee belong me!"

"Please—just until she's calmer."

Simon shrugged while Nicholas's dark eyes probed mine. Silently I pleaded, one hand protectively stroking the old lady's snarled and matted hair. I don't know why I reacted so strongly, perhaps only because the old lady had attached herself so firmly to me. It would have been cruel to have shoved her away.

"There's nothing you can do, Miss Farraday."

"Perhaps not," I snapped in sudden anger, "but there certainly was something the two of you could have done! If she doesn't leave the house, certainly you could have prevented her getting more of that infamous stuff!"

That shot went home. Simon's eyes glittered. "Don't you think we tried that? It only makes her worse. She yells the house down. Tonight is nothing to compare to it."

"No more talk. Time Missee come!" Once more Yu-Wei grabbed at Mrs. Berkley. This time it was roughly done, and the old lady and I staggered under the assault.

"Just a minute," Nicholas said, placing a restraining hand on Yu-Wei's arm.

She turned on him like an angry cat. "I look after Missee many year. Missee mine!"

Perhaps it was something in the way she said those last two words, but suddenly I could feel that both brothers were as revolted by her attitude as I. There was an evil glitter in her eyes that reminded me most unpleasantly of a cat with a mouse trapped and helpless between its paws.

"What do you think, Nicholas?"

"Mother certainly does take to the estimable Miss Farraday. If she wishes, I have no objection."

The Chinese woman made a hissing sound, for all the world like a cornered snake. "No one take care of Missee but me! I look after her long time."

"Then you should be glad of a small respite. Go to bed, Yu-Wei." Nicholas's voice carried an unmistakable edge of authority and, after a moment's hesitation, the small figure in the pants crept away. Mrs. Berkley began to sob softly against my shoulder.

"There, there," I said gently, stroking the heaving shoulders. "Come with me. Let's put you to bed."

"No," she cried weakly and firmly set her feet against moving, "not in there. No more. No more."

"Very well, then," I answered calmly, trying to humor her. "You will come to my room."

She meekly allowed me to lead her down the hallway and tuck her into bed. Nicholas and Simon followed, the expressions of concern on their faces thawing my heart toward them. They really did care for the old lady who was their mother.

Nicholas lit the candles by the bed and then, retrieving the box of vestas from the floor, lit the oil lamp on the dresser. In this glow of light and attention, I was suddenly very conscious of being clad in nothing but my nightgown and shawl. Of course, my nightgown was a voluminous garment with long sleeves and a high neck, but it was still a nightgown. Aunt Evelyn would have died of mortification.

"Will you be all right, Miss Farraday?" Simon asked.

"Certainly. I'm just going to brush out your mother's hair so she can rest more comfortably and then we'll go to sleep." I really had no idea of what to do, but that sounded like a good idea.

Nicholas laid a warm hand on my shoulder and despite my good resolutions, despite the situation, despite everything I could feel a glow rising through me. "We'll be just downstairs if you should need anything."

For a moment he smiled at me, and the world ceased to exist beyond the two of us. It only lasted a second, of course, then he turned to Simon and asked to see him in the library. The two of them left, leaving me feeling very foolish.

"Are they gone?"

"Yes, Mrs. Berkley."

With a speed and agility that was startling she dashed from the bed and snapped the lock on the door; a look of satisfied cunning filled her wizened little face as the bolt clicked home. For a moment I felt a thrill of fear at being locked in with a woman of such uncertain temperament, but her next words drove all thoughts but one from my mind.

"There, dear. They won't disturb us again like they did the last time." She cocked her head like a bird. "I knew you'd come back."

"Back?" I breathed, hardly daring to build a hope on the word of a madwoman.

"Yes, dear. I hope they didn't hurt you when they took you away." Her hand gently touched my face. "It's best not to fight them, you know. They always win. And then they hurt you."

The clouds crossed her face again, and she began to sob—small, quiet sobs that tore at my heart. I gathered her into my arms and somehow got her to sit down on the edge of the bed. Outside the wind sighed like a tired old woman as it moved slowly around the house.

"You said you were going to brush my hair," she demanded pettishly. "The captain loved my hair. He said it was like corn silk in the wind." Her laugh was a dreadful parody of a flirtatious giggle.

With a sinking heart, I began to gently brush her matted tresses. Perhaps once they had been the yellow of corn silk, but now they were grey and snarled so badly I could hardly separate one strand from another. She prattled on happily about the captain, about their courtship, and the good early years when the boys had been little. It was sad, but she was mad after all. Heaven only knew whom she had thought I was before, I thought in dejection. Then her voice changed and once again I listened carefully to her words.

"I don't think they'll be listening now. We can talk. I didn't know you were coming last time," she said. "I wasn't ready for you. They always give me more medicine in the autumn. If I want to think, I have to not take it, but then they put it in the food."

Medicine? What medicine? Good God, did she mean opium?

"Mrs. Berkley, are you saying that they force the opium on you when you don't want it?"

The ravaged face that had once been the beautiful Felicity Winterthorpe Berkley strained. "No, I want it. God in Heaven, I always want it. But it clouds my mind, and when I want to think or to talk I know I mustn't have it. Then they make me take it, and when I need it they don't give me any, they just sit there and watch me hurt. It's because of the captain, you see."

"The captain?"

"He was a man, you understand, and a man like that has appetites. Oh, I shouldn't be talking like this to you, but since you're going to marry my own dear boy, you should know—men are different." She eyed me wisely, and I would have sworn that she was as sane as I.

I nodded dumbly, the comfortable theory of her madness exploding at her words. There was no confusion; she had to have seen Doro, for in my tenure at Devon House my status had been unequivocally that of housekeeper, not of financée.

"I had never expected my dear captain to have been a saint, but he really never should have married that girl. He never would have if he'd known what grief it would cause me, but of course when he married her he hadn't even met me yet."

The whole thing was starting to make a horrible sense. "Did your husband insist that she become your maid?"

"Yes. It seemed the most sensible thing at the time. There was to be a child, you see, and the captain was very conscious of his responsibilities. Besides, he thought it would make a nice servant for the children we would have." She sighed and smiled with a ghastly dead pride. "I gave him two sons, you know; she only gave him one. That's another thing she can never forgive."

I bit my lips. That sanctimonious old Yankee! His bastard a servant for his legitimate children, indeed! In the South, a new-born child was given a slave of the same sex and approximately the same age as a birth-gift; this boy or girl was its companion and servant until death. There had been a great deal of criticism of this practice in the northern press recently; I wondered what those upstanding Yankee journalists would make of the same story enacted by one of their own esteemed citizens!

"Mrs. Berkley," I asked slowly, unable to wait any longer, "do you remember my name?"

"Of course I do, my dear. You told me several times before they took you away. You're Dorothea."

Chapter Fourteen

IT TOOK A long time for me to get the entire story straight. Mrs. Berkley was tired, and her abstinence from the drug was painful to watch; at times her mind wandered and at times she was incoherent, but at others she was as sharp as anyone despite the pains which racked her body. I could get no more information about Doro, no matter how I tried. It seemed that sometime in the past—she was very hazy about time—Doro had crept into her room and begged for help. They, whoever they were, had taken her away, and Mrs. Berkley had seen her no more until she had glimpsed me one day. In her mind I was still Doro.

Disappointing as that was, I kept at her, making her retell her story again and again until I had everything straight. She was tiring, she did wander in her mind from time to time, but her story never varied so that at last I was forced to believe.

Yu-Wei had not always been a servant. In China she had been a high-ranking daughter of a warlord and quite the beauty. Nelson Berkley had come to trade and been bewitched by the lovely Chinese girl. Apparently he had never been the kind to be balked in getting anything he wanted and, save snatching her away and probably starting a war in the process, there was no way of getting Yu-Wei short of marriage; so, marry her he did, according to the customs of her people.

Apparently the match was happy until the captain saw the fresh English beauty of Felicity Winterthorpe and determined to have her. Perhaps he had never regarded his liaison with Yu-Wei as anything but a dalliance in the first place, or perhaps he merely tired of his exotic wife, so the captain informed Yu-Wei that he was marrying the delicious English woman according to his customs, and that from now on Felicity would be his real and only wife. Yu-Wei apparently accepted this dictum, agreeing to stay on as the new Mrs. Berkley's servant so that the captain would take care of the child that was to come.

For a man who spent so much of his life among the Oriental races, the captain seemed to have an almost criminal lack of understanding of them. According to Mrs. Berkley, they set a great deal on face— sort of a combination of pride and appearances—and to lose face was worse than death. Yu-Wei could not go back to her family after such a disgraceful loss of face, so she determined her own revenge.

All was harmonious while the captain lived; he seemed to have a genuine love for Felicity, and she worshipped him. Two sons were born to them, and it appeared as if the old island woman's curse had lost its effect on Devon House.

Apparently Felicity had known nothing of Yu-Wei's past, save that at one time she had been the captain's mistress and that Chang was his son. Like a dutiful wife, she accepted gracefully what she could not change and tried to be good to the Chinese woman and her son. Then the captain died during the Opium Wars, and Felicity found herself at the mercy of her ancient and unknown enemy.

Yu-Wei insidiously began introducing her mistress into the ways of opium; gradually at first, then after the boys were away at school, dosing her so severely that days and weeks slipped by without her noticing, usually coinciding with the boys' visits home. Understandably, they began to find her drugged incoherence disgusting and began to avoid any contact with her that was not absolutely necessary.

One would think that such degradation was enough for Yu-Wei, but no; the Chinese woman had built up a store of hatred that had festered and become something hideous. She regarded herself as the captain's only true wife and Felicity a usurping concubine who must be punished for her presumption.

And punish she did. During the years Yu-Wei's madness grew as she fed her mistress opium and cackled over her in triumph. I thought that quite hideous enough, but there was worse to come. In the years of her supremacy, all the Chinese woman's frustrations and hatred came out; it was not enough to see her former mistress lolling in mindless stupor because of drugs or screaming in pain because the drugs were withheld, so Yu-Wei began telling her what she believed to be the truth, that she was the real wife and Felicity the concubine. This mental abuse kept up and grew and finally metamorphosed into blows. Yu-Wei's increased thirst for humiliation of her old enemy took the form of heavier and heavier beatings until finally Mrs. Berkley had resigned herself to death.

"She beat you?" I asked incredulously.

The old woman nodded solemnly. "She hasn't in the last few days, but then I've been getting more of my medicine. She doesn't like to hit me when I've had my medicine. You see, I can't feel."

Something in my expression must have spoken of incredulity, for without warning the old woman hitched up her nightgown to show me her back. It was crisscrossed with weals, some relatively fresh, some quite old. There were bruises that overlapped and dried, crusty scabs, and puckered scars. I had lived in what the northerners called a barbarous society all my life, but I had never seen such abuse on another human being, black or white. My stomach heaved.

"But what about your sons, Mrs. Berkley?" I asked skeptically. Surely they could not have condoned this hideous practice!

She was in bed now, her grey mane combed and respectably braided, and looking like any other elderly lady who has been ill for a long time. "My boys? They were never home much after they went to school. One lives in China, you know, and the other here, and they alternate. That's something the captain set up." Even now there was a hint of pride in her voice when she spoke of her dead husband. "He didn't want the two parts of the business ever splitting into two companies."

"But why wouldn't they help you?"

"I saw them so seldom, my dear." Ever the loving mother, she refused to believe ill of her children. "Whenever they are here, Yu-Wei increases my medicine until I don't know if it is day or night. Anything I say is taken to be a vision or a dream." Her hands knotted and she looked away. "Even when they are here they don't come very often. I disgust them."

"And how have you kept so clear-headed this time?"

"When you came before I promised I would help you, don't you remember?" she asked gently. Her soft hand patted mine. "Since I've known you were back I've only pretended to take my medicine and when they put it in my food or make me take it I make myself vomit afterwards. It's hard, especially when you're used to something . . ." she murmured, her face etched with a bleak hunger. "But it was my last chance."

I stood in awe of her. Not only had she endured mental and physical tortures for years, but she still had the strength of will to try and overcome a dreadful need that had been forced on her. And her sons had done nothing! Rage bubbled in my soul.

"Do you think you can sleep now?"

She nodded and snuggled down like a child. "Yes. It doesn't hurt so much now."

"Rest if you can, Mrs. Berkley." I stroked her forehead gently. "I've got to leave for a minute."

"You're going?" Fear flashed in those faded old eyes.

"Just for a little while. But I'll leave the lamp lit so that you can feel quite safe."

"She won't come get me?"

"She won't dare. I won't let her. Do you want me to lock the door behind me?"

The bravado of my words seemed to calm her, and she shook her head, lying back quietly.

I, however, did not intend to be quiet! I was going to give both the Berkley brothers a good piece of my mind!

All propriety forgotten, I again flung on my shawl and set forth, not even feeling the chill floor under my bare feet. Like a virago, I pounded heartily at both Nicholas's and Simon's bedchambers, determined to have it out with both of them, and was not a little put down when nothing but silence answered my knocks. Surely neither of them could have slept through all that!

I was not at all daunted. If they were in the house, I would find them. Such abuse of an elderly lady would not go on for one more minute if I had anything to say about it! In addition, I finally had a witness to Doro's presence in this house. Not even the skeptical Berkleys could refuse to believe me now.

Nicholas was in the library. There was only one lamp burning, and he had lit a small blaze in the ornate fireplace. He sat slumped in his chair, his eyes closed. He looked worn and weary and even through my anger my fickle heart went out to him.

He had looked asleep, but as soon as the door closed he opened his eyes, then jumped to his feet. "Miss Farraday! Is everything all right?"

"No, it is not." I was a bit hard in tone; I had no intention of letting his charm deter me from my purpose. How dare he have criticized the abuses in my homeland when such a criminal situation existed in his own house!

"Miss Farraday, you are barefooted! You must be frozen. Come sit down next to the fire, and let me get you a brandy."

Actually both things sounded quite enticing, but I was far too angry to be distracted by his blandishments. Not that he gave me much of a chance; I was all but shoved into the chair that he had just vacated and my feet unceremoniously propped on a footstool close to the fire. I hadn't realized how cold I was until the warmth began to penetrate my flesh, not a little helped by my fiery blush. Never since my infant days had a man seen my bare foot or ankle; I had thought myself above worrying about such niceties, but the thought of Nicholas Berkley's hands on my uncovered flesh gave rise to a whole host of extremely unladylike thoughts. Only my anger saved me from falling into complete incoherency.

"You are most kind, Mr. Berkley. What a pity you cannot show your mother the same courtesy."

He leaned back against the desk and regarded me with dark, unreadable eyes. It was an uncomfortable scrutiny.

"I told you about my mother. Simon and I both tried to warn you. I'm sure with your tender heart you meant well, but the situation . . ."

"You, sir, know nothing about the situation!" I took a gulp of the brandy he had pressed into my hand, the fiery liquid giving me courage.

"Strong words, Miss Farraday." His face hardened. "Dealing with an opium addict is seldom pleasant."

"So you avoid her all together."

"It seemed kindest."

"Kindest!"

"Doubtless she had told you how she cannot bear the sight of either Simon or me. She so resents our being alive when our father is dead that she dopes herself into insensibility rather than see us. Without my father her life has not been worth living."

So this was Yu-Wei's final revenge, the complete alienation of her rival's sons.

"That," I snapped, "at least is true." Then I proceeded to tell him the tale his mother had told me. Condensed it took but a few minutes, but those few minutes were enough for his expression to change to one of rage so black it frightened me, and I was but the innocent bearer of the news.

"It is incredible," he muttered. His eyes had become haunted. "To think that this has been going on . . ."

"Yu-Wei was careful that you saw just what she told you," I said hastily, alarmed no longer by the anger in his eyes but by the self-recrimination lurking behind it.

"Are you sure that this is not just an opium dream?"

I had to be fair. "No sir, as to the details I am not, but I don't think any opium dream could produce the scars that mark her back."

"Scars! My God. . . ."he cried in anguish, and I longed to rush to him, to comfort him. "I must go to her . . ."

"Please, not now. She's sleeping. She never stopped loving you, you know."

"And you cast salt in my wounds. But you're right. She deserves undisturbed rest and then all the tomorrows we can give her. I must tell Simon, and we must end this right away. Tonight! They must be gone by morning!"

For a moment the anger in his eyes blazed frighteningly, then died, and was replaced with a much more gentle emotion. He took my hands—I had long since discarded the empty brandy snifter and declined more—and kissed them gently, lingeringly; the touch of his lips was warm and gentle to my skin.

"Miss Farraday—Drusilla—you have rendered this family a great service, and at the moment I can do no more than say thank you."

Suddenly taken by an attack of demureness—a stupid condition from which I seldom suffer, thank heavens—I could only murmur, "It was my pleasure to be of service to you, Mr. Berkley."

Something flashed in his eyes. "That we will see, Miss Farraday." Then the moment of intimacy was gone, marked only by the rapid elevation of my pulse, and the darkness was back in his face. "I must beg one more favor of you; please go back to my mother and stay with her. Are you afraid?"

I cleared my throat and tried to bring my wandering wits back to the problem at hand. "Is there something which you think I should fear?"

"Yu-Wei will not give over her sovereignty easily."

"I will lock the door."

"Would you feel safer if you were armed?" He pulled open a drawer to reveal an exceedingly large and nasty looking gun. "Do you know how to use one of these things?"

"Yes, but for the safety of the house I should prefer not to," I answered firmly.

A flash of amusement crossed his face. "If you feel that way, certainly you had better not. Come. I'll take you upstairs."

Anger must have buoyed him, for he climbed the steps with no visible effort and, after silently checking my room for possible intruders, stood looking down at his sleeping mother. It was a touching scene, and, though it had come about by my intervention, I felt an intruder and looked away.

It was but a moment later I felt his hands on my shoulders; no, even though this was our only physical contact, I could feel much more. I could feel the nearness of his body, the tension that pulled at every muscle and sinew, even the pain beyond that of his wounds that pulled at his heart. I had never felt so close to another human being in my life. It was almost like drowning.

"Do you mind staying here?"

"No." It was a lie; I wanted to stay in that strange intimacy with him forever. I felt that if he pulled away it would be like removing a part of myself.

"Lock the door. I'll go wake Simon and we'll get this settled."

"Simon isn't in his room, I said, and instantly the atmosphere changed. He did not move his hands or his posture, but he withdrew from me as surely as if he had walked across the room. "It was so late I thought you had gone to sleep. I tried both your doors before seeking you downstairs."

"I'll find him or just take care of it myself, then. Be sure and lock your door."

"I shall."

He did move then, and I turned to face him. In the pale light of the low lamp, he appeared bigger and darker than ever, and, though I was glad of its outcome, I grieved that I had been the instrument of so much hurt. Then, without warning, he bent and pulled me to him, his lips seeking mine. I had never been kissed before, save for pecks on the cheek or forehead by sundry relatives and Simon's similar salute the previous day, and was totally unprepared for the flood of emotions which washed over me. My poor pen has no power to describe the upheaval within my breast, save to say that past and future both dissolved in the swirling joy of the present, and I found myself returning the ardor of his kiss with an enthusiasm that shocked me.

"Later, my little Drusilla, I have much to say to you," he said in an oddly husky voice and then kissed me again.

Mrs. Berkley was sleeping soundly, perhaps her first peaceful sleep in years. I hadn't the heart to disturb her, so I pulled the extra quilt—an aged thing which smelled slightly of age and mildew—from the armoire drawer and prepared to spend the night on the old fainting couch.

For a while I mused on Nicholas's extraordinary actions and how pleasurable I had found them, then wondered if at last I understood Doro's effusions in her last letters about her Mr. Berkley.

Such thoughts were a mistake; for all I knew—though I didn't really accept it for a moment—Nicholas was Doro's Mr. Berkley.

And where was she? Mrs. Berkley had confirmed my knowledge that Doro had been here, yet neither of her sons would admit even knowing her. By logic, that meant either Nicholas or Simon was not only a liar, but most likely a villain. It was a depressing thought.

Chapter Fifteen

I HAD VOWED to lie awake that night in case there should be trouble, but my body betrayed me, and I fell into a deep sleep peopled with phantom figures of terror. It was well past dawn when I awoke to the cheerful bustle of Mrs. Webber laying out a breakfast tray. A cheery fire in the tiny grate made the room quite comfortable, and the chimney hardly smoked.

"I thought it would be about time you were waking," she said. "Here's a nice cup of coffee to help get your heart started."

I sat up and stretched. My back seemed to have acquired several new angles during the night. "Good morning. I'm sorry to have overslept so badly." My eyes fell on the empty bed and for a moment my heart froze. "Mrs. Berkley! Where . . . ?"

"Ah, the poor lamb! Don't you fret about her. She's down in the library having breakfast with Master Nicholas and Master Simon as happy as you please. She's not over the worst of it by a long chalk, but right now she couldn't be happier." Pulling forth a large handkerchief and blowing heartily, Mrs. Webber all but beamed with pleasure.

"It's a wondrous thing you did, Miss Farraday. When I opened the door to check on you both this morning, she was awake and looking more like she did when the captain was alive. I could hardly believe it when Master Nicholas told me about it this morning." Tears misted her eyes as she draped a napkin over my lap and removed the cover from a plate heaping with delicacies.

"You opened the door? How?"

"There's a master key in the pantry. Always has been, from the time the boys locked themselves in the attic. Now you eat!"

So much for my simple faith in the protection of a locked door.

"Really, Mrs. Webber, you shouldn't have done this. I could have come to the kitchen."

Now she had started to make up the bed. "Nonsense, Miss Farraday! After what you've done for Mrs. Berkley, you're entitled to more than a bit of pampering. And to think of what those heathen Chinee have gotten away with right under our very noses!" She plumped the pillows savagely.

"What happened to them? Are they still here?"

"No, Master Nicholas said he took care of them. Sent them packing, he did," she said with a grim satisfaction. "Threw them out last night and said it would be worth their skins if the dawn caught them anywhere in his sight."

I tasted the eggs. They were delicious. Somehow I hadn't expected to be hungry, but I was ravenous. So Yu-Wei and Chang were gone, just like that. It seemed a shame that they received so little punishment in return for all the pain they had caused, yet one could understand Nicholas's reluctance to expose his mother to more grief.

"And they left?"

"Must have gone right away, for there wasn't hide nor hair of them to be found when I arrived this morning." Her face was alight with a grim satisfaction. "And as for Master Simon cutting up so when Master Nicholas told him . . . serves him right for believing that thieving Chang. He knew he'd been diddled fair enough, and it made him right furious."

"Nicholas acted without Simon?"

"Master Simon wasn't here. He came riding up as saucy as you please just as I was starting breakfast. Been out on business, he said. Humph! As if I couldn't guess that his business was probably with that Mrs. Harbottle what ain't any better than she should be." Mrs. Webber stopped suddenly, then turned to me, her face blanched. "I'm sorry, miss! I was just rattling on like I hadn't got good sense and forgetting that you are a maiden lady!"

I took a sip of coffee in an attempt to hide my smile. While I was indeed ignorant of the exact mechanics of such an indiscretion, the spirit of the thing was not unknown to me. It appeared that an interest in fancy pieces was just as prevalent among northern men as among our gentlemen of the South.

"It's quite all right, Mrs. Webber. Tell me what Simon said."

"Oh, at first there was a terrible row," she said, relishing every word. "I was serving them coffee while breakfast was cooking and they quarrelled as if I wasn't even there. Master Simon was all fired up that Master Nicholas had dismissed them without asking him, said that he had always been jealous that Chang begrudged serving him, said that he had no right. Then Master Nicholas told him what them heathen had done to their mother and Master Simon didn't say another word, but his face . . ." She shuddered. "Faith, Miss Farraday, I never saw such a look on a human face. Fair turned my blood to water, it did."

I could imagine. Nicholas's had had the same look the night before. One should think twice before angering either Berkley brother.

"Anyway, he was all for having it out with them right then and there. Looked like he would have flogged them to death, but of course by then they'd gone. Now miss, you've barely touched your breakfast!"

Indeed the plate was still more full than empty, but then originally it had held quite enough for a fair-sized family. "You fixed so much, Mrs. Webber! It was delicious, and I simply can't hold another bite. Thank you so very much."

"It wasn't anything, miss. Now Master Nicholas wants to see you in the library when you're dressed. He said I wasn't to rush you, but would you come to him first thing?"

Would I come to him? In truth I wanted nothing more. The memory of his kiss had been seared into my very soul, and I longed to fling myself at him with no thought of anyone or anything else. All that stopped me was the thought of Doro. Had he kissed her, too? Was he the Mr. Berkley of whom she had written so passionately? Or was Simon?

I hesitated outside the door of the library; suppose Nicholas did not echo my fine sentiments, but intended to treat me in accordance with my vulgar behavior? I tried not to think of my own reactions and opened the door.

"Mr. Berkley? Mrs. Webber said you wished to see me."

He had not slept. Still wearing the same shirt and trousers of the night before, now sadly creased and rumpled, he lay back in the great wing chair. Strain and weariness had sharpened the angles of his face and pulled the skin tightly over them. A bluish haze of beard clouded his chin and great dark circles stained the hollows of his eyes; his scarred cheek appeared to have been freshly branded.

"Drusilla," he said softly, and all my fears were banished.

He held out his arms, and I went into them as easily as if I had always belonged there. For once the image of Doro was not foremost in my mind, and I abandoned myself to the glory of his embrace. His lips sought mine as eagerly as mine did his, and for a few minutes there was nothing in the world but the two of us. Outside the brilliant autumn sunlight was a sham to hide the cold wind off the sea and the gaily multicolored leaves were but the harbingers of winter's darkness, but Nicholas and I stood wrapped in the glow of our own personal springtime.

"Please!" I said at last. "Your mother . . ."

"She's upstairs in my room and by now is probably sound asleep. Coming down for breakfast tired her considerably; we're going to have to be very careful with her."

"In your room?"

"Yes, Simon's chimney smokes, so I've been dispossessed again." A smile teased the corners of his mouth. How could I have ever thought it harsh and hard? "Aren't you sorry for me?"

Such gallantry should be rewarded, so in the interest of compassion I allowed him to kiss me again. In fact, I even helped. Enthusiastically.

"I didn't intend it to be this way, you know," he said at last. "I wanted to woo you with flowers and candy and Sunday rides in the carriage."

"Before or after I had finished my duties?" I asked tartly, and we laughed together as if we had been doing so for years.

"What did I do before you entered my life?" He stroked my hair gently. "I thought I should never laugh again."

The somber note in his voice colored the day and though I should have been flattered I could feel only remorse. It was selfish of me to be so happy when Doro's fate was still a mystery.

"Mr. Berkley . . ."

"Nicholas."

"Nicholas," I parroted with pleasure. "Doro was here. Your mother saw her."

"She told you that?"

"Yes. She thought I was Doro and that she had seen me before. She said that Doro had talked of escape. Nicholas, what has happened to her?"

I wished I could see his eyes. Often the truth of a person's words can be proven in their expression, but at the moment he was holding my head tightly against his shoulder.

"Mother mentioned having seen you before. I thought . . . Are you sure you understood her perfectly?" His voice was lifeless.

Inside I was beginning to grow cold. "She called me Dorothea," I said and pulled back. In my emotional turmoil had I made a mistake? "I asked her who I was, and she said I was Dorothea. Doro has red hair, too."

He smiled, but it didn't reach his eyes. "A family of redheads? I shall have to watch my step."

"Nicholas, what do you know about Doro?"

His smile faded. Now it was his turn to draw back. "Nothing, Drusilla. Nothing, but I have promised to find her for you. I have men looking all up and down the coast."

"I don't think she ever left here, Nicholas."

We stared blankly at each other.

"I must know she's all right," I said lamely, then added in hesitant little jerks, "I must be sure of that before I can think of anything else."

An awkward silence lay between us. Stammering like a schoolgirl I said something about finishing my work and fled the room, my cheeks ablaze. Had I not known before, this was proof that something was dreadfully wrong, and Doro was the key.

Chapter Sixteen

IT WAS LATER that Simon found me in the downstairs parlor, half-heartedly trying to gather up the grimy bibelots for a good scrubbing. It was fortunate that my quick bout with self-indulgent tears had run its course and that there was enough dust about to justify my reddened nose and eyes. When he first stepped into the room, it was an indicator of my preoccupation that my leaping pulse mistook his identity, and I very nearly missed calling him by his brother's name.

"Miss Farraday . . ." He shivered as the cool air of the room touched him, then grabbed both of his hands in my own.

"Please, Mr. Berkley, I'm all over dirt . . ."

"You're all over ice! You shouldn't be working in here without a fire."

"I shan't be here long. I'm just gathering these up." I gestured to the trayful of figurines and what-nots. "Besides, the chimney is fouled with birds' nests. They've even fallen through onto the grate."

"I'm not surprised. This old place is going to rack and ruin. I hate to see you wearing yourself out on it."

Such concern touched me. "You're too kind, Mr. Berkley."

"Nonsense. If I were really kind I should not permit you to work here at all. I—come, sit here." Without releasing my hands he guided me to the spindly old settee. Little clouds of dust rose around us when we sat down. "Do you remember, Miss Farraday, that I asked you to let me help you, that I wanted to be your friend?"

"Yes, Mr. Berkley, you have been very kind to me."

"I don't know how to begin. . . . Please don't take this wrongly, but I must caution you that you are in grave danger!" His hands were almost painful on mine. "I saw you and my brother this morning."

My voice refused to work, but I fear my face was all too eloquent. I could feel my color draining away, then rushing back to glow like a sunset.

"How prettily you blush, my dear Miss Farraday!" he said gently and the teasing tone was just right to allow me to regain my equilibrium. "I didn't mean to, you know. I opened the door and he—he was kissing you. Neither of you heard me, so I thought it best to withdraw."

I appreciated the delicacy of his action and started to say so, but he forestalled me.

"Please listen to me. If I didn't have your best interests at heart I would keep silent, no matter my own desires, but . . ." He faltered to a halt and his face fell as he read my expression. "I had no idea it had gone so far."

"I appreciate your concern, Mr. Berkley, but I must make my own judgements."

"Damn Nicholas!" he said with sudden venom. "Always running in first, always grabbing . . . I'm sorry, Miss Farraday. It's just that I held back before, trying to restrain myself, trying not to rush you. I never dreamed Nicholas . . . Anyway, I must speak my mind!"

I had a dreadful premonition. "Please don't."

"I must. I've thought about it for days now. Soon I'll be leaving for China. The *Evening Star* is almost ready. Come with me, Miss Farraday—dearest Drusilla. Let me take care of you."

For an awful moment I thought he was going to embrace me. How strange that though the two brothers were so outwardly similar, the thought of being caressed by one was exhilarating, but by the other held no excitement at all. At least this proposal had been made in the accents of a gentleman, without any of Jack Howard's histrionics.

"I appreciate your offer, Mr. Berkley, but I cannot accept."

"Then there is nothing I could say to change your mind?"

"I'm sorry."

"I am, too, Miss Farraday," he said in a tight little voice and left me abruptly.

For a moment I felt quite guilty for having dashed his hopes, then began to look at the situation more rationally. I could not feel that he cherished any grand passion for me; in fact, I had a sneaking suspicion that my main attraction for him was that his brother seemed to want me.

Had he made similar advances to Doro?

I sat down and pressed icy fingers against my aching head. No matter where my thoughts led, everything came back to Doro. Where was she? And how was I to find her?

As have many before me, I sought solace in hard work and joined the crew in Mrs. Berkley's suite. Whatever the Chinese woman had been doing these past years, it had not included housekeeping. The rooms were a pigsty.

Mrs. Webber had lit an enormous fire, flung wide the windows to the cold, fresh wind, and taken an unholy pride in scrubbing the place from one end to the other. She was surprised when I took the heavy brush from Maud and attacked the floor myself, but wisely let me be, knowing that sometimes hard work was the best way to solve a problem.

"Are you all right, Miss Farraday?" she asked once as I brought yet another bucket of water up the stairs. "Everything seemed so fine this morning."

"I'm all right, Mrs. Webber," I replied shortly and returned to my scrubbing. "There's nothing to worry about."

That didn't stop her from worrying, of course; it showed in the way she kept looking at me the rest of the day, in the way she chided me to go down to dinner as requested instead of hiding in my room with something on a tray. Even my offer to have dinner with Mrs. Berkley was vetoed as she had already eaten and by then was probably asleep. According to Mrs. Webber, she would sleep a great deal at irregular hours, and she was not to be disturbed unless she wanted company. Mrs. Webber was adamant, so I had no choice but to accede.

Dinner that night was, to say the least, a strained affair. Outside it was quite as gloomy; the sky had clouded over just at sunset and before it was full dark a slow, steady rain had begun to fall. At least I didn't have to worry about Mrs. Webber going home in the rain. She had appointed herself nurse, guardian, and protector to Mrs. Berkley and had moved into the house for the time being.

Dear Mrs. Webber! If only she had known of the discomfort to which her insistence had committed me. Nicholas and Simon sat like ghosts at the table, each ignoring the other; equally silent, I sat between them and wished I were somewhere else. Mrs. Webber served the dinner herself and from course to course she could tell that things were not as they had been; her distress was visible.

At last the ordeal was over. We spooned up the last of Mrs. Webber's rice pudding and then sat in dreadful silence. I rang the service bell once, but when she did not appear I began to stack the dishes myself, my attention on the two brothers. So different and yet so similar! Yet one sent my pulses racing, and the other inspired no feeling beyond mild friendship. Had Doro felt the same way? Had she thrilled to Nicholas's kisses? Or had it been Simon who had wooed her so tenderly? How could I think of anything or anyone until I had found Doro?

The dishes rattled dangerously in my hand.

"Miss Farraday! Don't you worry with those. Here, I'll take them." Efficiently Mrs. Webber whisked the tray from my hands. "I'm sorry I'm late, but Mrs. Berkley wanted a cup of tea, bless her. And, Master Nicholas, she asked if you could see her for a moment."

"Of course. I'll go right up," Nicholas answered and, holding the door for the burdened Mrs. Webber, left me alone with Simon.

It was a confrontation I had hoped to avoid. Simon seemed to be as uncomfortable as I, so I stood to go.

"If you will excuse me . . ."

"You don't have to run away, Miss Farraday. I shan't embarrass us both by repeating my offer." Simon smiled gently.

"I don't wish to make you uncomfortable, sir. Perhaps it would be best if I went on upstairs."

The firelight turned his eyes to a dull gold. They looked sad. "I won't try to keep you, though I do wish you would forgive me."

What could I have done? To have departed then would have been churlish at best, so I smiled somewhat uncertainly and sat back down. "There is nothing to forgive, Mr. Berkley. Please don't think of it again."

He nodded politely and turned his attention to the desk where a large napkin swathed a bottle. It had been there since we had come down to dinner and, knowing the Berkley cellars, I should have been quite interested had I been less preoccupied with my own problems. His fingers twitching nervously, Simon peeked under the edge of the napkin, then, letting out a low whistle, lifted an ancient and crusty bottle in reverent hands.

"Good Lord! I haven't seen a bottle of this in years. I didn't know there was any left in the cellars. Look."

Lured by curiosity, I peeped over his shoulder to see a fabled vintage for which Uncle Miller happily would have traded his wife and children. I had heard of such a wine, but had never dreamed to see it and said so.

"Nicholas must have planned a celebration in Mother's honor," Simon said, pointing to the silver tray where the bottle had rested and the three heavy crystal goblets beside it. "The bottle is even open to breathe." Simon sniffed the bottle and licked his lips appreciatively. "That aroma! Dare we?"

I took a whiff; it literally made my mouth water. "It seems a shame not to wait for Mr. Berkley."

"He might be hours with Mother. I don't think he'll leave her until she goes back to sleep."

The wine's fragrance crept out of the bottle like a djinn to dance tantalizingly under my nose. "It is nearly time to retire . . ."

"Perhaps just a small glass? We could save the rest for tomorrow."

I nodded, happy to let myself be convinced. Perhaps this exquisite wine would sweeten the end of a very distressing day. More foolish was I for thinking so.

Simon insisted on making a little ceremony of it. I returned to my chair, and, napkin over his arm in the time-honored custom of wine stewards, he poured two glasses and handed me one.

"May I give you a toast, Miss Farraday? To happiness, both for today and in the future."

"To happiness, both for today and in the future," I repeated. Our glasses resounded with a clear note as they touched. "A lovely toast to go with a lovely wine."

"And a lovely lady," he added with a carefully impersonal gallantry. Still, it made me uncomfortable and only my excitement about tasting such a storied vintage kept me from fleeing there and then.

My first disappointment came when I held it up to the firelight. Instead of the pure, clear color of old stained glass, the wine was dark and cloudy.

"It's been addled! Oh, look!" I cried in disillusionment.

The second disappointment was the taste. Underneath there was the rich full body of fine old spirits, but the bouquet was slightly bitter. It threw the whole taste off.

"Something wrong, Miss Farraday?"

Somehow I felt like a child when a promised treat has been denied. "It's just not as good as I had thought it would be."

Simon sniffed his. "Tastes quite good to me. Try some more."

I drained the glass, but my opinion did not change. "I suppose it's just outlived its prime. What a pity."

"It still tastes fine to me." Simon finished his glass and poured another. "Maybe that's one of the blessings of an indifferent palate; everything tastes good. Sure you won't try some more?"

"No, thank you. I really think I should retire now. If Mr. Berkley should return, would you apologize that I was unable to join both of you in your celebration?"

"Of course. Miss Farraday . . ."

I paused at the door. "Yes?"

"It's nothing," he said after a moment, but his eyes were sad, and he stood in the library door watching until I was out of sight upstairs.

Chapter Seventeen

THE RAIN CONTINUED to fall steadily, creating a solid curtain of water outside my window. I watched the drops bead together and run down the pane; in the dim lamplight they glittered like little eyes. Beyond the glass there was nothing but the darkness. No moon could pierce those thick, soaking clouds, and darkness that surrounded Devon House like a blanket.

My nightgown clasped in my hand, I sat dully on the edge of the bed, too tired even to undress. I had not been conscious of working so hard today, but perhaps the strain and fatigue of the past week were beginning to tell. My limbs felt like lead weights and, conversely, my head felt light, as if, at any given moment, it might float away from my body. I hoped I was not becoming ill; if I were sick, who would search for Doro?

Doro! Where was Doro? Leaning my head against one of the carved bedposts, I could have cried in sheer frustration. For all the success I had had in locating her, she might as well have been snatched by the Devil, as Abijah had said those other girls had been.

I yawned convulsively, the effort making my head swim. Indeed, I must be sickening for something. A good night's rest . . . My fingers fumbled with the buttons of my basque and, finding the task too much for them, fell useless in my lap. I studied them in dismay for a moment, until my consciousness itself spun away into the darkness, and I fell senseless across the bed.

Something unpleasantly cool lapped at my face and I shivered. "Oh, she moved!" cried a girlish voice. "She's waking up.'"

Indeed I was, and the process was extremely unwelcome. I was not particularly comfortable lost in a black haze, but I had a pretty fair suspicion that my situation would not be improved by consciousness. As feeling slowly crept back into my extremities, I was aware of nothing but discomfort. I was lying on something hard and cold and to confuse my disordered senses even more, there was a thread of voices. Wherever I was, I was no longer in my room.

"Oh, Dilly, please wake up!" the voice pleaded, and, in spite of myself, my eyes flew open. Only one person had ever called me that.

"Doro?" I croaked hoarsely.

Even in my present condition, I should have known the answer to that immediately. I could also tell why my appearance in Port Harmon and Devon House should have caused such a stir, for to look into the face of Dorothea Conroe was like looking into the mirror at my own.

I struggled into a sitting position and looked hungrily at her face. Not only did we share the same mane of fiery hair, our faces were the same oval shape and possessed the same tip-tilted nose that freckled on the slightest exposure to the sun. Her jaw was firmer and more square than mine, for it has always been affirmed among the Farradays that I have my father's jaw, but our lips might have been taken from the same mold. Her eyes were the opaque green of a summer pond where mine have always been considered more hazel, but we both possessed the same dark brows.

It is an upsetting thing to one not born a twin to see your own face on someone else and especially when that face showed the unmistakable marks of abuse. Yes, my darling Doro had been severely mistreated. Her hair was a great snarl, the bones of her face stood out under a thin covering of pale skin, and a great bruise discolored one whole side of her face. She was painfully thin and her dress was filthy. Weeping for her pain, I embraced her.

Later I noticed our surroundings. It could only be a cave, for the floor, walls, and ceiling were all of rough rock which fairly streamed with water. A few rickety wooden cots lined the walls, each covered with a pitifully thin blanket. A small window looked out onto the open ocean and admitted a prodigious amount of cold air. Iron bars, clumsily set in rough concrete, sealed off the natural entry to this tomb. Through them I could see another chamber much like this one and a narrow, winding passage worn in the rock. The ceilings were low, the floors uneven, and the only light came in through the small window, giving the whole horrible scene a dreamlike dimness.

It was not my surroundings, however, that sent the greatest thrill of horror through me and still brings nightmares on occasion; it was the poor creatures who shared my captivity. Their dull eyes looked on me with no real spark of either interest or pity, and I realized with a sinking heart, I had found not only Doro but the ten missing girls of Port Harmon.

"Doro, how came I here?" I struggled to a standing position and was forced to lean against the chill, dank wall as the world revolved madly around me.

"He brought you, of course. Just before dawn." Her voice was dark with bitterness. "Just dumped you on the ground as if you were a sack of meal. Oh, Dilly, you slept for hours and hours! We tried, but we couldn't lift you onto a bed. We weren't strong enough." Now her voice quivered and threatened to break. Tears edged her bloodshot eyes.

"Please don't, Doro. You mustn't blame yourself." Gently I pushed myself away from the wall. The world still whirled, but I could stand.

"I thought you were dead!" Doro cried and burst into tears. "He told me you were here, he told me what he was going to do to you. He knew how it would hurt me."

I placed my arms around her sob-tossed shoulders, amazed at how prominent her bones were, and somehow managed to guide her to a cot. Doro's distress was easy to understand, and I grieved for her; to know a loved one is in danger and be unable to help is the worst torture there is. I had felt a small part of it, but how much more dreadful it must be to know each step of the plan and be powerless to give aid. The fatal question hovered on my lips and cowardly I pushed it aside.

"Doro, I have no memory . . ."

"They gave you a drug," she said, daintily wiping her eyes on her skirt. "In your wineglass. He told me all about it. You just thought the wine was addled. It was a sleeping drug, one that's very common in China. It works fast and leaves no ill effects."

I could attest to that. Even the dreadful swimming feeling in my head was fading fast and I felt fine physically. Emotionally—emotionally, I was in a fury.

"They drug our food," she continued in a colorless tone. "We tried doing without, but there's never enough and . . ." Her hands flopped helplessly in her lap. "He doesn't want us to be strong or to think. These poor girls have had more than I. He cut down on my dosage so that I could appreciate what he was doing to you."

The man was a monster! The Devil did indeed walk in Connecticut, and I could no longer hesitate about exposing him despite my personal feelings. "Who, Doro? Who is he?"

"Mr. Berkley." She looked up at me, her dull eyes awash in guilty tears. "My own dear Mr. Berkley!"

That in itself was not surprising. I should have liked to have it rest there; surely the man's identity made no immediate difference in effecting our escape from this hellhole, but some demon drove me on. "The same Mr. Berkley who courted you?"

"He said he loved me." Her lower lip trembled until she caught it between firm teeth. "And I believed him."

"What was his first name, Doro?" I asked, my mouth tasting of ashes. "Which one was he?"

"Which one? There's only one Berkley. Nicholas. Nicholas Berkley."

I used to think of death as a singular thing, a simple ceasing, a passing from the world of men into the world of the Father. In that moment I learned that there are many kinds of death, and the cruelest is when the spirit is quenched, leaving both body and intellect well and functioning.

So I had been deceived and—I had to admit—willingly so. I would have defended Nicholas to the death without the evidence of Doro's word. Now the death involved well might be my own, for I had no intention of sitting here until I too could be drugged into a zombie!

I began to breathe normally again, and anger, consuming anger, was my salvation. The hurt and the pain and the sorrow could be examined and endured later when the work was done; it would keep for now.

"Dilly, are you all right? You looked so strange."

I took a deep breath. "I'm all right," I said and my voice was harsh. Poor Doro didn't understand, for she looked even more distressed and asked what was wrong. "Nothing," I replied more gently, "except that I have been quite as foolish as you. It must be part of our heritage."

"I don't understand."

"I'll explain later, Doro. Right now you must help me."

Once again her hands flopped helplessly, and her eyes filled with tears. "I can't," she moaned. Such faintness of heart was totally inconsistent with the high-spirited Doro who had written me for years; it had to be a result of the drug, and that made me the more determined not to take any.

"Doro! Help me! I must know what is going on here! Why are we here? What is the reason behind all this?"

Dull green eyes looked into mine, their depths full of horror. "Don't you know?"

"Of course not, you ninny! If I knew, would I be asking you? Doro, you've got to help me!"

"There are men in the Orient—men who like white girls," she said in a small voice. "There is one who wants a redhead."

I felt as if I had been struck. A number of melodramatic reasons for Doro's disappearance had occurred to me, but nothing this horrible, this unbelievable. This was the stuff of nightmares and Doro had been facing it for weeks. Suddenly the oblivion of the drug seemed a blessing.

"And now he has two."

She nodded slowly. "He told me you were a redhead."

And that monster had had the nerve to criticize our southern form of servitude when he was engaged in a much more dastardly enterprise! "Doro, do you know when we are to be taken over there?"

"I don't know." She shook her head slowly. "We were in the house until a short time ago. Mr. Berkley said that we would leave, then there was a great commotion, and we were brought down here. We've been here ever since. I'm sorry, Dilly," she cried, the tears welling again. "I can't remember . . ."

I comforted her mechanically. Her information had indeed been scanty, but I thought I understood it. Now I knew why those deserted rooms had been strangely clean. When I had arrived the girls had been hustled down here; I couldn't quite figure out why I had not been taken immediately—some refinement of cruelty on the part of that dastardly Nicholas Berkley, no doubt—but since I had been taken, now the time of our removal from these shores could not be far off.

That meant I had to act quickly! Leaving a sobbing Doro on the cot, I made a swift inventory of the room. It was a little eerie moving among the four girls who shared our cell. I had never believed the tales the servants told of voodoo and zombies, but I must admit that these Yankee girls, immobilized by a drug from halfway around the world, made me think twice about those old legends. The blank eyes of the remaining six from the other cell seemed to look right through me. It was an unnerving experience, as if I were alone in a world of shades.

I peered through the tiny window, compressing my shoulders as much as possible, but still they stuck against the rough stone. Giving a yank that cost me a rent in the arm of my mistreated gown, I pulled back. It was foolish to think of escape that way, which is why our captor had neglected to have it barred. Perhaps one of the others . . . ?

A quick glance around disabused me of that notion; there were one or two who were frail enough to fit through that opening, but even if the way outside had been smooth, they would have been too drugged to be of any use.

Besides, there was no place for them to go. There was a caldron of rocks and water below the window that boded certain death for anyone foolish enough to attempt escape that way. Above the window was a bulge of rock that hid everything but the sky from view.

"You can't get out that way, Dilly," Doro said dully.

"Is this where you threw your bertha?"

Surprise flashed across her face. "You found it, then?"

"Yes," I said shortly, lacking the courage to tell her that it was the finding of her bertha which had condemned me to share her fate.

"We threw everything up there that we could spare, handkerchiefs, petticoats, caps. Most of them just fell into the water and ended up on the rocks."

"What made you throw your bertha that day?"

She shrugged. "It was the last thing we had."

"And the things in the house?"

"You found them?"

How could I tell her of the hope and frustration those few personal articles had caused me, of the searching they had inspired, and of the grief I had felt when the searches proved fruitless?

"Yes."

"I hoped someone would. I couldn't just do nothing!" Her face contorted with agony. "But I never thought it would be you, Dilly! I never dreamed you would be caught. I'd give my life if you weren't . . ."

She was becoming hysterical. I clasped her hands tightly. "Hush, Doro! We'll get out of here. . . ."

"There's no way, Dilly. We've tried everything. We're trapped." Doro's voice was bleak with despair.

She might think that, but I was not so easily cowed. God in Heaven, if I ever got my hands on that sweet-talking cad I'd horsewhip him! My anger gave me energy, and I scurried around the cell like a hound on a scent.

The walls were virgin rock; this cave was obviously as old as time. I thought of the tales of wreckers and smugglers. Once I had merely thought them legends, but now I would believe anything of the Berkley clan.

And yet . . .

The female mind is indeed a wondrous thing and never more so than when it is bedazzled by love. Even as I boiled with rage against him, my frail heart began to look for flaws in the story. If it indeed were Nicholas who had wooed and betrayed Doro, why had she never mentioned his infirmities in her letters? They must have been much more pronounced then, yet she had never said a word.

No, I decided, balancing on a chunk of rock to inspect a promising chimney that almost immediately dwindled to nothing. More likely, in the first flow of love, she had merely ignored his injuries, much as I had almost ceased to see them after getting to know the man himself—if I had ever really known him. It was a small thing, but, even after I had reached that decision, it continued to nag at me.

I rubbed the cement at the bottom of the bars. It was rough, grainy, and, given sufficient pressure, rolled away under my fingertips.

"These were clumsily set," I muttered.

"We tried that, Dilly," Doro replied in a mournful voice. "We scraped at it until our hands were raw. It didn't do any good."

The girls stared as I fumbled under my voluminous dress; my cage-like woven extension skirt dropped to the ground and I thanked heaven for dear Eula. It was difficult for my bare hands to free one of the springy metal bands from its casing of tape and even more so to wiggle it back and forth until the dainty brad holding the two edges together gave way. At last every obstacle fell before my determination, and, thanks to the French modistes and my modish empty-headed cousin, I had a tool!

When I started scraping away at the most lightly encrusted of the bars, the others finally understood. A dull murmur of approval arose, and I realized that I had just given them the one thing that might overcome that dreadful drug—hope.

I dug and scraped at the mortar until my hands were swollen and bleeding. More than half the bar was exposed, but I could do nothing more and that frightened me. In this dim hellhole there was little concept of time, yet I knew it was passing, and with each moment gone we were one moment closer to our captor's return.

Even if he did not discern my attempt at escape, he would doubtless drug us.

Then Doro responded. She took the misshapen metal from my battered hands and began to scrape at the mortar with a concentrated fury. Her drugged state made her movements weak and unconcentrated, but she persevered, her skill improving as the anger and the exercise began to drive the effects of the sedatives from her system.

An agonizing length of time later, the bottom of the bar was free. The other girls helped now, their clumsiness a drawback, but among us we managed to push and pull that bar until the mortar at the top released its hold, and the bar came free in our hands.

"Dilly! You did it! We're free," Doro cried with joy, but I wasn't so sure. First of all, we had indeed removed one bar, but the resultant space was exceedingly narrow. Two of the girls might make it through with ease, yet were they in any shape to cope with the unknown in that rock corridor?

No, it would have to be I who squeezed through there, and a squeeze it was going to be. Aunt Evelyn had always said my appetite was disgracefully healthy for a lady!

It was a difficult maneuver and accomplished only by an assisting push from Doro, but at least I was out—at the cost of several more rents in my dress and a painful collection of scrapes and bruises. All the more, I thought, to be charged to the account of Nicholas Berkley!

The light had faded badly without our noticing. It was nearly dark in the hall. I crept forward slowly, hugging the wall for whatever protection the shadows might give, every sense alert for any danger. Without the extension provided by the metal cage, my skirts clustered thickly under my feet; I had to carry most of the excess under one arm to be able to walk without tripping, and this made me clumsy. I was also hungry; I hadn't eaten since the night before and by now it must be at least mid-afternoon. Perhaps in my present situation I shouldn't have thought of such a trivial matter, but when one is hungry it isn't so trivial! I ignored the rumblings of my stomach and edged on carefully.

This was the most hazardous part of our escape; if I were to be caught here there could be no recourse. I would be captured, reimprisoned, and there would never be another opportunity. All of us would be loaded like cargo onto a ship and taken across the world to a land of carved dragons and . . .

Something brushed my hair, something thin and cold. My mind conjured tales of skeletal hands, and I struggled not to run in screaming terror. "Don't be afraid until you have something to be afraid of, girl!" Great-aunt Lorena had said time and again, but it was difficult advice to follow when alone in a shadowy hall, fleeing a villain, and feeling icy fingers in one's hair!

After an inner struggle of some magnitude, my old training came to the fore, and I calmed down enough that I could breathe. With shrinking fingers I reached upward and disentangled myself.

It took a moment before I realized just what a boon fate had delivered into my hands, for the icy fingers clawing at my hair had been nothing more than two long keys hung on the wall!

This indeed was freedom! Ever conscious of the seconds ticking away, I raced back to the cells and wasted time fumbling with the great primitive locks, but at last both crude doors swung open. I dashed to the small window and flung both keys as far as I could into the sea. If I had anything to do with it, these smugglers' caves would never imprison another young woman!

"Come!" I commanded the others. "We must get out of here."

In truth, I didn't have much of an idea where to go; my order was merely an atavistic desire to escape, to leave this place of horror behind. Obviously we could not go back to Devon House; even if I could guarantee that Nicholas would not be there, I could not face those sneering dragons again. Even if Chang and the dreadful Yu-Wei were gone and the house empty, I never wanted to walk through those portals again.

But where to go? The town was too far; I wasn't sure I could walk the distance myself and the others surely couldn't make it. The Webbers? Every nerve in my body said that the Webbers were decent people with no knowledge of this atrocity, but until a short time ago I would have said the same thing of Nicholas Berkley. No,

I wanted nothing to do with anyone connected with Devon House, not the Webbers, not anyone! If there were only someplace safe where I could hide the others while I took a horse and rode into town for help, or if luck were with me I could get the wagon hitched and take us all out of here.

One of the girls started to whimper; I could hear Doro comforting her. By now the passage had grown uncomfortably dark and the rough floor sloped treacherously uphill.

"Wait a minute. I don't want any of us spraining an ankle." I spoke with the surety of authority as my mind was reeling with a sense of my own inadequacy. It was too dangerous for these weak creatures to continue in the dark, but it would only get darker, and each moment we spent here was that much more dangerous.

"Dilly . . ." Doro's voice skated on the edge of hysteria. "We can't stay here. We've got to get out!"

"Well, we can't go on in the dark, can we?" I snapped with a lamentable lack of patience. I knew Doro's whining was the effects of the drug, but it was beginning to annoy me. Then, as I was mentally railing at her for being so witless, the obvious truth hit. If we could not see in the dark, neither could he!

"Doro, when did he bring you your food?"

"He never did. He only came down here to gloat. It was always that Chinese devil." She shuddered, and I could not imagine how dreadful it must have been for her to have this constant reminder of her ultimate fate paraded before her.

"But what time? Day, night—when?"

"Anytime. There was no schedule." Her attention drifted to one of the girls who was openly crying, but I had to have an answer.

"Did they ever come at night, Doro?"

"Sometimes," she answered absently.

If they had come at night, there must be a lantern somewhere, as I didn't think that Chinese could see in the dark any better than we. Leaving the girls huddled against the wall and cautioning them to be quiet, I inched forward, my hands becoming my eyes against the rough stone. Fortunately the floor was relatively smooth despite the sharp upward slant, and there were no steps to trip me.

The light was fading, whether from natural evening or from our distance to the window. I didn't really know and didn't really care; the fact that it was getting darker was enough. The idea of being stuck deep in the dark bowels of the earth, of being many feet underground with no sight of God's own sky, brought forth inner terrors more suited to a child in the nursery than a woman of eighteen years.

And yet even these nightmares paled next to the unimaginable horrors that awaited us if we failed to escape.

That thought sent me forward even faster, my feet shuffling against the rough floor, my fingertips beginning to be scraped raw by the gritty wall. Then, abruptly, the wall beneath my hand was no longer there and I stumbled, nearly falling. What was this? Was it a tunnel to the surface, a route to the house, or a room? In the dim murk I could make out nothing more than a patch of black slightly darker than the surrounding air.

For a moment I debated which way to take, then decided to continue on; should this route prove fruitless, I could always return. I hoped.

The floor slanted upward even more sharply now and I was groping forward in nearly total darkness. I was considering the wisdom of turning back when my fingertips, now scraped almost raw from the stone wall, made painful contact with a door.

After that it was fairly simple. There was a shelf that held an ancient shielded stick and a box of wax vestas. Normally a single candle does not yield much light, but after the Stygian gloom it appeared as bright as a beacon.

In a few moments I had cause to wish it wasn't so revealing.

The door beside the candle shelf was very firmly locked, and I could find no way of opening it, of course; any keys would have been on the other side. It was a heavy door, ancient and solid, and then I knew where I was. This was the other side of the mysterious door in the cellar, the door that covered nothing but a walled-up passage. The absurdity of that story was equalled only by my arrogant folly in accepting it so unquestioningly!

I heaved a sigh and wearily started back down the passage, which strangely seemed smaller and more close in the light. Our last hope was the other open doorway. I could only pray that it led to the outside and was not just a room. If it were, we should have to attack the door and, if we could get it open, risk discovery by our noise, or wait until it was opened and try to overpower Nicholas. Rather, I should have to, since none of the others could do much more than hold themselves erect. Even with his infirmities, Nicholas Berkley would be more than a physical match for me. Neither option was very enticing.

I tried very hard not to think of the last time Nicholas Berkley's hands had touched me. How innocent I had been then! And, if anyone had told me then of his perfidy, would I have believed them?

It was a much shorter trip returning to the opening than it had been going; in the dark those few yards had seemed endless. I wished it had been longer.

At first glance it seemed an answer to a prayer; there was a tunnel, narrow, twisting, and leading upward, but I gave it no more than a fleeting glance. My eyes were riveted on two figures in a small alcove in the rock.

I had jumped, thinking them to be alive; it was nothing to see them in Devon House, so still as to be just one more of their heathen carvings.

This was definitely, horridly different. I saw that almost at once. Crumpled like discarded toys, Yu-Wei was doubled over against the wall, and Chang, his eyes dusty and staring, leaned against her in an obscene parody of an attentive rag doll. They had been dead for some time; the blood that had gushed from their slashed necks and soaked their tunics had dried into thick puddles.

If I had needed more proof of his villainy, here it was. Had I not seen the flashing anger in his eyes when I had told him of the Chinese servants' treachery, and had he not promised most solemnly that they would be gone before morning? He had even told Mrs. Webber that he had "handled everything." The crusted blood seemed to glow dully in the candlelight.

I could not let the others see this! Such a sight would overset their poor, tortured nerves immediately. I looked for something to cover the bodies, somehow sinister even in death, and found nothing. Instead I had to rely on my wits, and, after fetching Doro and the others up that long dark stone tube, tried to use my body and the shadow it cast to hide the grisly sight.

I think it worked, but the passage was so narrow that to allow the others to pass in single file I had to stand so close that Chang's dead hand, stiff and horribly cold, lay against my ankle. It was a sensation that would give me nightmares for years.

At last we were past that obstacle and, after some maneuvering, I was once again leading my little band forward, trying to forget what lay sightless and rotting in the dark behind us. This time luck was with us. Although our way was blocked with a very solid oaken door, it opened with no great amount of effort to reveal a thicket of bushes and a wide expanse of sullen, rain-laden sky.

We had escaped!

Chapter Eighteen

WE PUSHED OUR way through the screening bushes and shivered as the chill wind raked at us. I didn't know what was worse; the dank, pervading cold of the tunnel or the tearing cold of the wind.

"Why don't you and the others wait just inside the door?" I suggested to Doro. Their long imprisonment had left them weak; there was no need to court them catching their death of the grippe or the ague. "I've got to see where we are."

They all voted that idea down with fervor. They would crouch in the lee of the bushes, but they refused to reenter that dark hole.

"We thought we'd never get out," Doro said. "We won't go back."

I could not argue with them. Besides, from the look of the sky, it was fairly late in the afternoon, and there was a goodish storm building up. Whatever we were going to do had to be done quickly; night and storms were more than I could contend with at the moment.

Cautiously I poked my head out of the bushes. There were a lot of them and quite thick—almost a copse choked with underbrush— and once I could see the surrounding country clearly, I understood. This was the edge of the wood near the gates. We were well past the narrow neck of the peninsula and not a hundred yards from the stables! Unfortunately, that hundred yards was all open; we would be exposed the entire distance.

"Dilly, what are we going to do?"

I should have been powerless had I been alone; my nerve would have failed, and I should have been found eventually, huddled in shocked exhaustion in the brushy copse. The trust and the dependence of the others, however, thrust on me a courage and energy I should never have had on my own. They had suffered too much, endured too much, not to escape now.

"I am going to get the wagon. You and the others will wait here, Doro. I'll come for you when everything is ready."

"Dilly, please be careful."

It was perhaps the most useless advice ever given. What had to be done had to be done, no matter the risk. Reassuring her the best I could, I gathered up the bulk of my skirts—wishing that I could have the freedom of a costume like Yu-Wei's—and prepared to dash across the open area. If I could just get the wagon hitched and the girls into it with no one seeing . . .

A tall, lean figure stepped into the barn doorway, elegantly flicking the dust from his sleeve, and for a half second my heart stopped until I saw his cheek was unmarked.

"Simon!" I called joyously, unaware until I had spoken that I had used his Christian name.

He looked up, an expression of shock freezing his features. It was to be expected; scratched and dirty, with my hair halfway down my back and my skirts hiked up to my knees, I must have made an exceptional picture running across the grass. His paralysis only lasted for a moment, then he was running toward me and I was wrapped in his long, strong arms as he restlessly scanned the area for any apparent danger.

I had never been so glad to see anyone in my life. Completely forgetting all propriety and modesty—as if anything Aunt Evelyn had ever taught me could cover this situation—I leaned against him, feeling his strength, happy to put my burdens on his broad shoulders. Wasting no more time, Simon scooped me up in his arms as if I were terribly precious and hurried with me toward the shelter of the gate wall, placing his own body between me and whatever lurked beyond.

"Simon, oh, Simon. I found Doro and all the others. They're being kept like animals in cages. We've got to get out of here. . . ."

His restless eyes never stopped searching for any sign of movement. "Where are they now?"

"Over there. There's a door leading to the underground caves. They were locked in cages, like animals!" I gestured wildly toward the copse. "We've got to get out of here, we've got to get them to town before Nicholas comes back!"

"Nicholas?"

"Yes. I wish I could have broken it to you more gently," I said quickly, slightly bemused and frightened by the strange expression twisting his face. In my fear I had forgotten that this monster was his brother—his brother, whom I had chosen over him. "But it is Nicholas who has kept those girls down there. They're to be sold like animals to a Chinese lord."

Overhead the thunder rumbled, sounding to my overwrought senses like the growling of a stalking dragon. A drop of rain, thick and wet, splashed against my cheek. The trees bent even further under the advancing wind as if they too were trying to escape a terrible fate. The sky hung so low I could almost have reached up and touched it.

"How did you get out?"

It took a moment for the import of his question to sink in. A slash of lightning arced to the ground, its quick glare giving Simon's chiseled face the look of a wolf.

How had he known I was in, unless . . . ?

"You're part of it," I said slowly.

He flashed a merry, charming smile. "I am 'it,' dear Dilly," he said, the use of my pet name confirming his confession. No one but Doro had ever called me that. "Now we must put all of our pretty birds back in their cages. Lord Fang-Ti wouldn't like it if either of his little redheads was damaged. Your coming was such a stroke of luck, Dilly," he smiled, stroking my hair as if it were an ornament. "I expected a reward for finding old Fang-Ti a redhead, but when I deliver two, I shall be a great man. You two will be the pride of his house."

"And the others?" I asked with fascinated horror.

"They will go to men with less discriminating tastes—or smaller pocketbooks."

"And you would just sell us, like so much meat? Have you no honor?"

"Surely you can appreciate my position, Dilly. After all, you will be well treated. No one in their right mind would mistreat a valuable asset, and you will live in a much more civilized atmosphere. I'm sure he will regard you as one of the family. Think of all you can learn!"

How odious of him to quote my own words back to me when the meanest intelligence could see that the situation was not the same at all!

"You are a monster!"

"Hardly; merely a businessman."

"You did it all," I said in amazement. It had been obvious all the time, if I had only had the wits to see it. "You wanted to take me away under your protection and when that didn't work you asked me to . . . Oh, infamous! To ask me to go with you as your wife when you intended . . ."

"It would have been easier," he laughed. Taking my wrist he tried to drag me forward, but I struggled, determined to put off until the last possible moment the ultimate defeat. I would die before being taken to that hole in the ground and the unspeakable hell that lay beyond.

"And the time the horses bolted . . . You threw that stone."

"It was no trick to circle the town and catch up with you. I had hoped to scare you away from the house, so no one would question your departure. And, before you ask, I did send the company assets to China in Nicholas's name, but they were deposited to my account."

His comment set off a whole new train of thought. Nicholas—Mrs. Webber—they would question my disappearance, and I proclaimed this while scratching wildly at his imprisoning hand.

"Hardly. Did you think me so careless?" He grabbed my other wrist with insulting ease and rendered me helpless. "You have run away, my dear. You regretted your reckless behavior and the thought of allying yourself to a scarred cripple revolted you. You left a note for my dear brother that was quite graphic."

145

For the first time my courage failed. Nicholas would not be coming to my rescue. What was worse than that, he would spend the rest of his life thinking that I had crudely rejected him. The grief for his pain almost equalled that for my own situation.

Yet still I struggled. He would not get me back in those cages; instead I would die fighting for my freedom.

"You killed Chang and Yu-Wei."

"Of course. After what they did to my mother, what else could I do?" His eyes glittered and he licked his lips as if remembering a favorite flavor. "Though it was a pity it had to be so quick. In their homeland I learned there are slow ways of killing, ways that fit the crime . . ."

"You are a beast!" I said in feeling tones. "Cad! Dastard!"

"Language, language!" he replied teasingly, and his grip on my wrists became painful. "Now let's go find the other girls."

Great-aunt Lorena used to say that whatever the situation, you would be given strength to deal with it. In this case, it was not strength, but pure blind rage. I would not be locked up and sold like a prize cow! Using the advantage of surprise, I twisted one hand free and clawed at his face while my foot made solid contact with the sensitive part of his shin. I'm sure it was more being startled than anything else which made him loose his deathgrip on my other wrist, but it gave me the opening I needed. I yanked free and ran out into the open just as the rain began to splatter down.

I had forgotten my skirts. They bunched around me, grabbing my ankles, getting under my feet, and, after a frantic stumble, sent me thudding heavily to the ground. Struggling both to get my breath and get back on my feet, I could feel the reverberations of heavy footfalls behind me before Simon's hand latched onto my shoulders and pulled me upright.

"Now, Dilly, we must be sure that old Fang-Ti's merchandise isn't damaged."

"I am not merchandise!" I screamed, lashing at him with ineffectual feet and fists. This time he was prepared for my puny violence and I had no effect.

"Damn if you aren't exciting!" he breathed and his eyes glowed with some inner fire. "Not at all a proper nothing like your cousin. It's damned tempting to keep you for myself."

"Nicholas!" shrieked a feminine voice, and I had to look to see that it was Doro.

Dear, timid, half-drugged Doro! She had not been able to stand the suspense of waiting and had looked out of her safe shelter just in time to see me fall. Now, her weeks of imprisonment boiled over and she became a screaming Valkyrie bent on revenge. She flew forward and, like a swarm of dazed ghosts, the girls followed her, shambling on weakened limbs, their abused bodies driven by determination, their fists upraised in righteous retribution.

And then I understood at last. Even in this light there could be no mistaking the two brothers, especially not with eyes honed by loathing. Simon, with his deadly cunning, had used his brother's name as either a safeguard or perhaps as a refinement of hatred. In Doro's case, he had run little risk of exposure, as they would be unlikely to meet socially, and, at a distance, even taking Nicholas's wounds into account, it would be easy to mistake one for the other. The other girls had probably been simply taken when they walked alone; it was only the specialty of a redhead that had to be worked so carefully. Ladies of Doro's class didn't walk alone in areas where they could be easily taken.

In spite of everything my heart leapt. I had not been wrong! Nicholas was innocent.

The next moment proved it.

From behind us came the thunder of hooves, rivaling the rumbling of the sky in their urgency. Nicholas, a strangely vital, active Nicholas, flung himself to the ground, and, with one well-aimed blow, felled Simon. The girls clustered around him like harpies, flailing his unconscious body with moth-like blows from ineffectual fists. It was a scene from a nightmare, as if they were avenging spirits bent on destruction, but I could not stop them. I would have joined them before doing that; they had earned that pitiful revenge.

"Are you all right?" Nicholas asked anxiously, whipping the cloak from around his shoulders to drape over my soaking form. "Did he hurt you, darling?"

"He used your name," I said stupidly. "I thought . . ."

His arms went around me. They were safe and warm, and I felt so protected. "I meant you to, Drusilla," he said, misunderstanding me completely. "I had to pretend to be crippled until I could find out what he was up to."

"And you thought I cared about that?" I asked scornfully. My fingers touched his scarred cheek. "Or that this would matter?"

There was much more to say, things that it could take the rest of our lives to say, but at that moment words seemed utterly superfluous. Nicholas held me tighter, and, in the glory of his lips pressing passionately against mine, I forgot all else.

We were not allowed our selfish heaven for long. There were other hoofbeats and shouts and the tragic keening of the girls as they were pulled away from Simon's limp form. For all their hatred they had inflicted remarkably little damage on him—which I think was better than he deserved—but the catharsis of violence doubtless did a great deal for their poor, battered souls.

Nicholas had been at the head of a small band of riders. I recognized one or two of them as townsmen, staid and sober citizens by their dress. Webber was there, too, his weather-worn face creased with strong emotion. Mr. Wallingford rode with them, leading a few burly fellows whose awkward seat on a horse only underlined their appearance as seamen. It was with a distinct start that I recognized one of the riders. By now, I should have been inured to any surprise, but the sight of Uncle Richard, here in New England, astride a horse that could only be a rented hack, almost completely overset me.

"Drusilla, my girl! Are you all right?"

I laid my head against Nicholas's strong shoulder. "Now I am, uncle." I said contentedly. "Now I am."

Epilogue

ODD HOW THOSE long-ago days seem so close. Sitting here on my lovely flower-shaded balcony in the Singapore house to which Nicholas brought me as a bride, it seems as if only days instead of decades have passed since we left New England.

Still, even the passage of time cannot quiet some memories. I remember Simon's face, contorted with rage as he discovered his dire deeds unmasked; I remember his fury at the promise of a trial for the murder of the two Chinese and our kidnapping; I remember the curses he hurled at his brother before breaking free of his captors and hurling himself from the cliff edge to the cruel rocks below. Simon's death was ugly and cowardly, but at least Nicholas was spared the agony of a lengthy public trial and of seeing his family name forever tied to an executed criminal.

Even before leaving China, Nicholas had suspected his brother of being involved in something underhanded and had pledged his support to the search for the truth. So, much of his illness and weakness had been feigned in an attempt to lull the evildoers into thinking that he was harmless.

That fateful morning, Nicholas found the vicious note Simon had left to cover my abrupt disappearance; luckily for me, he didn't believe a word of it. Nicholas then set out for town to organize a search. He had heard of the smuggler's cave beneath the cliff, of course, but thought it had been sealed years ago. It had been, but the wily Yu-Wei had opened it, and it was there that Simon had indulged in other nefarious practices that had doubtlessly contributed to the fatal warping of his character. Nicholas had the caves blown up so that there could never be a repetition of this horror. As a result, the narrow neck of the peninsula collapsed, leaving Devon House aloof and alone on a tiny island accessible only by boat.

The day after, Nicholas asked me if I wished to return home. I said no. I could never return to the South. Living in a society based on slavery was now completely impossible for me; it would revive too many memories of that dreadful time when I had thought myself lost forever. I could never live with my conscience by condoning such a system any longer.

The poor darling man looked dreadful. His face was grey and he looked exhausted. The scar on his cheek was blood-red. I wanted to take him in my arms and comfort him.

"How are you feeling?" he asked.

"I'm all right. I feel rather silly lying here when there's so much to be done."

"Don't be gallant, Drusilla. Everything is under control, and you must rest." His fingers gently traced the line of my jaw, leaving a trail of fire in their wake. My heart pounded unbearably. "You've had a dreadful time. It was selfish of me to keep you here when I knew it was dangerous." His voice was bitter.

Now I recognized what was wrong. Too much had happened, Nicholas had borne too much shock and grief in the last two days; his sense of honor demanded expiation for his family's crimes, so the poor misguided darling was taking the blame upon himself. It was all very honorable and very genteel and, in my mind, very stupid.

"Don't be such a fool," I said tartly. "You couldn't make me leave when I came here and didn't know a thing about you. Do you think you can make me leave now that I love you more than anything on earth?"

"Are you sure, Drusilla?" he asked hoarsely. "It won't be easy. There will be a scandal. . . ."

"Don't you love me?"

His answer to that was swift; pulling me to him, he pressed his lips firmly against mine until I felt our flesh would become one, and the breath be crushed out of me.

"Damn you, woman, how can you ask such a question? I've loved you since you appeared in the hall, all dirty and angry and your hair halfway down your back, and started giving us orders. You are the most beautiful, most exciting woman I've ever known. I just want to protect you."

Men and their damnably complicated codes of honor! Had I not been so comfortably wrapped in his arms I could have stamped my foot in vexation.

"Well, it seems that as my husband you could do that quite well," I ventured and was happy to hear a chuckle and a whispered "Vixen!" Then, to seal his fate, I added, "Of course, if you want me as your concubine, I suppose . . ."

"Witch!" he cried and once again kissed me thoroughly. "We'll have nothing like that in this family again. You will be my legal and proper wife as soon as I can arrange it!"

"Yes, Nicholas," I said. "Most happily!"

In time both Doro and Mrs. Berkley came to live with us. Doro married a British trader, and to this day we are as close as sisters. Nothing could ever repay Mrs. Berkley for those dreadful lost years, yet I like to think that her time with us was happy. Perhaps in seeing her grandchildren grow, she found some slight recompense. I made peace with my own family and later helped some of them begin new lives after the holocaust of the South's attempt for independence.

Devon House has never been lived in since we left. It still sits there, empty and forlorn, gradually crumbling into a ruin. It was only the other day, when I first thought about writing down my fantastic tale, that I realized the old island woman's curse had come true. The Berkley family prospers, but the cheerless grey hulk of Devon House is doomed to decay and destruction.

I for one don't miss it a bit.

If you have enjoyed this book and would like to receive details of other Walker romances, please write to:

Judy Sullivan Books
Walker and Company
720 Fifth Avenue
New York, NY 10019